# WHITE EAGLES
# OVER SERBIA

# WHITE EAGLES OVER SERBIA

## Lawrence Durrell

ARCADE PUBLISHING · NEW YORK

FIRST ARCADE EDITION


*Library of Congress Cataloging-in-Publication Data*

Durrell, Lawrence.
     White eagles over Serbia / Lawrence Durrell. —1st Arcade ed.
        p.   cm.
     ISBN 1-55970-312-1
     I. Title.
     PR6007.U76W48    1995
     823'.912—dc20                95-17743


Published in the United States by Arcade Publishing, Inc.
Distributed by Little, Brown and Company

10  9  8  7  6  5  4  3  2  1

BP

PRINTED IN THE UNITED STATES OF AMERICA

# CONTENTS

# WHITE EAGLES
## OVER SERBIA

# CHAPTER ONE

## *The Gift of Tongues*

Though Methuen usually lived at his Club whenever he was in London it was seldom that he was seen in the bar or the gaunt smoking-rooms. This afternoon in June was something of an exception—and he surprised himself when he found that he was crossing the marble staircase by the porter's lodge, to push open the swing doors which opened on the private lounge. He was in search of congenial company, he told himself, and added under his breath, "And I am not feeling very particular." Four months in the jungles of Malaya had starved him for the sound of his own language and he was glad—yes, glad—to catch sight of old Archdale, the bore of bores, in one corner of the room. "You've been away a hell of a time," said Archdale mistily, out of his gold-rimmed monocle, and Methuen warmed to the familiar greeting. "Welcome back to the camp-fire, old man."

The camp-fire was in fact burning rather low and Methuen drew attention to it, as well as giving an order to the steward, before he sank into the arm-chair facing Archdale. They chatted idly for a while, and Archdale was really putting himself out to repay the sense of gratitude he felt for Methuen's company by retailing one of his longer stories, when the latter suddenly felt that he was being watched. He turned round in time to see the reflection of Dombey glide across the hall mirror. "O dear," he said, "I do hope Dombey isn't looking for me." Archdale gave a satisfied chuckle. "Well, it's not me he's after."

Methuen drank deeply and said by way of explanation: "You see I've just left him. Just reported and was given indefinite leave after this Far East show."

He looked nervously over his shoulder again and saw the doors open to admit the heavy dilapidated-looking figure of his chief—Dombey with the ant-eater's profile and the threadbare Old Etonian tie. He stood inside the door and pointed his long nose in Methuen's direction. "It is me," said Methuen sadly; but in order to make sure he waggled his hands interrogatively and pointed at himself. Dombey nodded slowly, smiling, and shuffled into the far corner of the room where he settled into a chair like some great bird and folded his great hands in front of him on the mahogany table-top with a gesture of a man closing a dossier. His half-closed eyes gave him the appearance of being perpetually dozing; an innocent owlish smile played upon his features. "Damn him," said Methuen vindictively, finishing his drink. "I'd better go and see what he wants." Archdale gave another fatuous chuckle. "What a life you chaps in the 'Awkward Shop' have. Thank God I have never been co-opted for that cloak-and-dagger stuff. Simple gunner. Suits me best."

At that moment it would have suited Methuen as well as anyone; Malaya had heartily sickened him and he was looking forward to a fortnight's fishing on a river he knew in Ireland. Dombey hung over these plans like a shadow. "How the devil," said Archdale testily (for he was loth to lose the only bit of company that was likely to come his way that afternoon), "how the devil do you *get* into that damned Hush-Hushery of Dombey's, eh?" Methuen answered in a voice pre-occupied by private regrets: "A gift of tongues in my case." "I see." He stood up and finished his drink: "They discovered I could talk languages." Archdale settled himself more firmly and said: "Parley vou francay? Thank God I never had any languages." Methuen coughed and braced himself: "Well, old man," he said with genuine regrets, "so long." Archdale made a sad little gesture and his monocle fell out. "Maybe it's nothing," he said hopefully. "Come back afterwards and I'll finish my story. It'll amuse you." "Thanks. If I can." Methuen picked his way across to Dombey's table like a man walking over a mine-field. "Ah!" said Dombey sleepily, "I was looking for you."

"I've just left your office, remember?" said Methuen acidly. Dombey nodded carefully, consolingly. "I wasn't ready to talk, then," he said. "Sincere apologies." Methuen lit a cigarette and said: "I'm on leave now. Remember you telling me?" Dombey made a soothing gesture in the air like a magician stroking a cat. "Yes," he agreed. "Of course you are." Then he fell silent for a good minute and studied his huge hands.

There was something distinctly Oriental about Dombey's personal approach to matters of business; he would skirt the subject which preoccupied him for ages before coming to the point. He would start, so to speak, at the furthest point from what he intended to say and work circuitously towards the point of impact which was always encapsulated in the phrase: "I just want you to go and have a little look." This he uttered in the oily tones of a Pasha soothing a creditor. He would begin, for example, by saying: "Any idea what the mean summer temperature of Baffin Land is?" or else "How far would it be from Rome to Geneva for a bicyclist?"

In this case he remained silent for a long time looking at Methuen with an air of reflective sobriety before he said: "How far would it be if one walked from Belgrade to Salonika?"

Methuen was used to this approach. Despite Dombey's high rank in the unit known to a few highly placed officials as SOq or Special Operations Q Branch, he was Methuen's junior by a number of years; and it was abundantly clear that you could not have a career as meteoric as Dombey's unless you had brains to back it. The slow and tortuous approach was not that of a slow-witted man; rather it was the approach of a man whose life-work consists in the fitting together of elaborate jig-saw puzzles in which the separate pieces were made up of intrigues, follies and human lapses: of dangers and alarms which beset the stability of British policy or design.

"Belgrade to Salonika?" said Methuen. "It depends how you walk. I personally would not and if that is what you are planning for me. . . ."

Dombey began to purr. "Wait," he said. "My dear fellow, don't rush me. Wait a second."

"I know your tricks," said Methuen severely, "and usually I don't mind. But really, Dombey, this last job was terribly tiring. I must have a rest."

"I promise you," said Dombey solemnly, "that I only want your advice. *Nothing will be wished on you.* Of course I would like you to go, I won't disguise it. But for the moment I only want your advice, see? Maybe the trip will appeal to you! How do either of us know that?" He sighed and sank back in his chair.

"What about Danny and the Professor?"

"No," said Dombey and shook his head decisively. "Enjoyable as it is to send you off together this is no territory for the three-ringed circus you make. It's a lone job, and as far as I can see, a damned difficult one. Of course I won't have you considering it as *your* job. I'll assign someone else. But your advice would be invaluable."

Life, thought Methuen to himself, was getting boring at SOq. The last three of his missions (with the exception of the Malayan one from which he had just returned) had been enlivened by the two friends he had named. Three was certainly better company than one when it came to high adventure, and the three oddly-assorted men had shared a number of exciting experiences together in various parts of the Balkans. But this was a lone job. . . . Well, the lone jobs had to be done by someone. Behind the resentment he felt (for he could see quite clearly that Dombey was baiting the hook for him), he felt also the sluggish stirrings of curiosity. He would at any rate like to know what he was refusing. "What is it all about?" he said at last, and Dombey stood up abruptly like an angler striking. He lit himself a cigarette and stretched out his long arms. Methuen sat looking up at him soberly. "Just give me a brief outline," he said, "and then I can clear off to a theatre."

Dombey blew out the match and stood up, exhaling a long streamer of smoke through his nose. "I can't talk clearly unless I'm in front of a map," he said. "Are you free now?" He must have seen the slow resentment in Methuen's eyes, for he caught his arm and said: "Let's go down to the 'Awkward Shop' together. I have everything arranged there." Methuen stood up and sighed. "One condition," he said. "I'm not leaving for anywhere before next Friday." Dombey made a large accommodating gesture in the air with his two arms. "But of course. But of course," he said almost plaintively.

The two men walked slowly out into the grey London dusk, arm in arm, like bondsmen, and crossed the Mall towards Charing Cross Road, talking in desultory fashion; darkness was falling as they reached the anonymous square where, in the shadow of the Seven Dials, Special Operations Unit lived and had its being. A duty clerk sat sorting letters on a green baize table-top. The darkness had closed in by now and Methuen, gazing up for a moment at the smoke-blue night sky, caught a glimpse of the battered angels which ornamented the roof of the building, riding there in the darkness like twelve ancient figure-heads. The building had once housed a Victorian insurance company, and the incidental sculptures which decorated its massive and now dirty cornices were eloquent reminders of the artistic criteria of the '90's. It was a strange flavourless barrack of a place, full of cold corridors and cramped lifts.

"Okay, sir," said the duty clerk, setting aside the wooden hurdle and admitting them to the darkened hall where they stood for a minute while he groped in his safe for the tagged keys to Dombey's office. The lift was, as always, out of order. They walked down a long corridor, turning on the lights as they went, and thence climbed the two floors to Dombey's office in silence. Vaguely from the dark depths below them, where the radio section lived, there came the tapping of static in a receiver, knocking on the darkness with monotonous iteration like a finger-nail on the surface of a drum. From behind a half-closed door on the first landing leaked a smear of fluorescent light which turned from purple to green and went out. Dombey fumbled with the door and threw it open with a crash.

Together they walked into the warm carpeted darkness of the room, and Methuen paused in his tracks to give his chief time to find the switch to the desk-lamp. How well he knew this room; it had been the starting-place of so many adventures. Mentally he built it up in all its detail, which the bright green desk-lamp would confirm: bookcases, the little mahogany bar, the stacks of map-cases, the camp-bed and the dictaphone with its rolls of wax stacked like ammunition on the shelf behind the desk. Dombey snapped on the light and as he did so delivered himself of the pregnant word: "*Yugoslavia.*" Methuen groaned and fumbled for another cigarette before stretching himself out in an arm-chair. "I know," said Dombey soothingly. "I know."

He took off his coat and crossed the room to the wall where the thick stack of maps stood, each in its stout cellophane-covered frame, and each attached to the wall by a brass member so that the series could be turned like the pages of a book. With his large white fingers Dombey leafed his way through Austria, Istria, Slovenia, and worked his way south towards Serbia. "You know the political background, Methuen," he said, "so I won't try and describe the Communist dictatorship of Tito. You were at Bari, weren't you, when the war ended?" Methuen nodded.

"Ever been back to the place since?"

"Not since fifty-three or thereabouts."

"How is your Serbian?"

"It used to be very good once." He had suddenly begun to watch Dombey's right hand as he might have watched the hand of a hypnotist. A vague image was rising in the back of his mind of high flushed mountains, crested with firs, and resonant with the vibration of icy waters flowing southwards and westwards. Dombey's finger had begun to quest among the mountains of southern Serbia, vaguely, irresolutely. It settled finally on a town in the old Turkish Sanjak of Novi Pazaar. Methuen smiled and sat up. It was as if a doctor had pressed upon an aching place. "Around here," said Dombey, and Methuen felt the province throb in his memory like a sick member.

"Twenty years ago or more," he said aloud, "I fished that whole range two years running."

"Something is going on here, in these mountains," Dombey paused impressively and lit himself a cigarette.

"What is the brief?"

"There isn't anything as clear as a brief."

"Where do I come in?"

"I don't know yet."

The noise of the London traffic murmured outside the window, imitating the ripple of trout streams in Methuen's imagination. "Explain," he said patiently, and Dombey began his explanation.

"We know the Royalists are working night and day to start a revolution against Tito. Their headquarters is in Paris and they are managing to infiltrate people into Yugoslavia. That's easy to understand. But recently, Methuen, they've been sending in small groups of fairly heavily armed people. Of course they don't stand a chance against Tito's OZNA organization; they are being gathered in like rabbits. There have been a dozen spy-trials in the last few months, all fairly openly reported in the Tito press, and all concerned with bands of *armed* men who are alleged to be roving about these mountains with some pretty decent equipment."

"War surplus bought in France?"

"Yes."

"But this is very normal for the Balkans."

"Nevertheless, *why* always in *this* area? It is easy to seal off this mountain chain. If you or I wanted to bother Tito there are a hundred likelier places to send agents to. Why get so many chaps captured and lose so much equipment in this place particularly? We don't know."

"What do the people on the spot think?"

"They are completely blanketed. Movements of foreign embassies are restricted to an area of twenty kilometres around Belgrade and Zagreb. Everyone is followed night and day. It is quite impossible for a foreigner to make an excursion into this area and see for himself."

"Perhaps they want to blow up the railway."

"Would there be any point in that?"

"None that I can see."

Dombey picked up a bundle of pin-flags from the tray on his desk and began sticking them on to the map at various points. "Seven different points in the same area," he said at last, standing back and putting his head on one side. "Now here's *another* thing. There has been of course a great deal of police activity in this area, but no great *military* movements, so obviously the Communists don't regard these incursions as any great threat to the stability of the régime. Nevertheless they themselves are as puzzled as we are."

"How do we know that?"

"Two refugees who worked for OZNA have recently come over to Trieste."

"Are you suggesting," said Methuen, "that I go wandering into this area and get myself bumped off as an agent of King Peter?"

"No," said Dombey. "I just want your advice."

"Could I reach Belgrade? There may be some gossip to be picked up there which would explain it."

"Would you like to?"

"If there were a chance of fishing those mountain streams I'd like to very much," said Methuen candidly, "but to sit in Belgrade and embarrass the Embassy. . . ."

"Ah yes," said Dombey sadly. "The Embassy." In general SOq made a point of operating independently of Foreign Office establishments abroad, in order not to compromise their work. "This is an exception," said Dombey sorrowfully. "I'm sorry about it. So by the way is Sir John. You should see his telegrams. He is dead against your going in. And frankly I'd prefer to operate independently. You could go in as a business man, but visas take an age to come through. I am anxious to push on with this show immediately. Particularly since this last accident. That has worried everyone." He paused.

"Ah!" said Methuen. "At *last* we are getting to the point. What has, in fact, happened?"

"Peter Anson is dead."

"Ah!" said Methuen soberly.

"You never met him. He was Military Attaché in Belgrade, and a keen fly-fisherman. He found a way of spending his week-ends in these mountains, and last week he didn't come back from a trip. Yesterday the OZNA notified the Embassy that they had found his body in the mountains near Novi Pazaar. Shot through the head. By one of these roving Royalist bands."

"But how stupid of him", said Methuen angrily, "to go blundering into an area like this with his trout-rod. I suppose he drove down there in his car, followed all the way?"

"No. He was cleverer than that. You see every week a car is allowed to take a bag down to the Consulate in Skoplje. The road passes through this area and there is a place in the valley where the OZNA car drops behind a good way. Peter used to drop himself off the car, spend Sunday in the mountains fishing, and pick up the car as it returned at dawn on Monday. Only this time he didn't come back."

There was a long silence. Dombey seated himself behind his desk again and began to draw on the green blotter with a pencil. "You see," he said softly, "why there isn't any brief? All this may be quite unworthy of our attention. Peter was of course trying to get in touch with one of these Royalist bands to find out what they were up to. It is quite likely that the Communists are telling the truth. He may have made contacts, only to be shot up by them. You see, the Royalists hate us nearly as much as the Communists do. They consider that we put Tito into power and were responsible for the death of Mihaelovic."

"I know," said Methuen wearily.

"Will you go as far as Belgrade. *Not* into the mountains, please. Just spend a week or two there and see what you can pick up. I shan't worry if you find nothing. The whole place is under the blanket."

"How would I go?"

"The War Office is sending out a civilian accountant to inspect their establishment there. His visa has been cleared.

You could go as Mr. Judson if you wished, and stay for a week or so."

"All right," said Methuen without any marked enthusiasm. "It's a thankless task. Hated by the reds and blacks, distrusted by the Embassy. . . ."

"Above all, no dicing with death," said Dombey, rubbing his nose. "Don't take chances."

"What does the Ambassador think?"

"He is livid with rage. But the Secretary of State is for us this time so he can't actually stop you."

"When do I start?"

"When can you?"

"I want a week. I shall ask Boris for a brief on the territory. You won't mind?"

"People don't read files any more," said Dombey plaintively. "They always go and see Boris."

"He should be on your staff really."

"If there were any justice in the world he should have my job," said Dombey. "But he prefers to make wigs."

"He's a good deal more rational than either of us."

"Yes," said Dombey sadly. "Yes."

"I'm getting old," said Methuen suddenly, standing up. "I can't think why having once retired I shouldn't end my days in the south of France or somewhere nice. Why keep on like this?"

"You would die of boredom."

"I suppose so."

"And by the way, if you don't like this job you have only to turn it down and I'll assign someone else."

"*Who* else?" said Methuen not without some pardonable contempt. "Is there anyone who knows that part of Serbia as well as I do?"

"Let us not become boastful," said Dombey, and he took

from his pocket a roll of galley proofs covered in erasures and blotches, and spread them before him gloatingly. "At least if I retired I should have a consuming interest to keep me sane." (He was the proud author of a monograph entitled "Aberrations of the Chalk-Hill Blue *Lysandra Coridon*".)

"Butterflies," said Methuen contemptuously. "I'll bring you back some butterflies to knock your eye out. You should see them in those mountains, settling in clouds along the rivers."

"Remember," said Dombey sternly. "*No* mountains. *No* rivers. You are not to go wandering off or I shall get hell from the Foreign Office."

"The Foreign Office!"

To his surprise Methuen found himself feeling all of a sudden extremely youthful and spry. He recognized the familiar feeling of heightened life which succeeded every fresh call to adventure.

"Damme if I don't walk over and see Boris now," he said, and he was already walking briskly across towards Covent Garden before he realized how skilfully Dombey had baited the hook for him; he was probably sitting up there in his office now, smiling, clasping and unclasping his great hands. Methuen felt the idea of Yugoslavia skidding upon the surface of his mind like a trout-fly, tracing its embroidery of ripples. He had risen right out of the water. "I shall certainly take my trout-rod," he muttered as he marched along. "Whatever Dombey says."

# CHAPTER TWO

## *Boris the Wig-maker*

Boris Pasquin's little shop was locked when Methuen reached it, but there was a light at the back of the building so he rattled the letter-box loudly and shouted "Boris" through it. The little theatrical wig-maker very seldom left the premises and there was a good chance that he was in the great rambling workshop at the back busily engaged in polishing a stone or playing patience.

In the gloom the crammed shelves of the showroom guarded their mysterious treasures—enough to delight the heart of a magpie or a child, for Boris combined his wig-making business with that of a general dealer in everything from precious stones to playing-cards. He himself was fond of saying that there were two hubs of the Empire, one official and one unofficial. The official hub was of course Piccadilly; the unofficial was Boris Pasquin's little shop in Covent Garden. This was something more than a flight of fancy for the range of Boris's interests did extend to practically every country in the Commonwealth.

While he had the kind of talent which goes to make millionaires he preferred to deal in small ranges of rare objects which delighted his imagination more than they profited his pocket. Shelves of china; Japanese fans; Byzantine metalwork from the marts of Salonika and Athens; statuettes smuggled from the "digs" of Egypt; hand-painted playing-cards from Smyrna; pages of illuminated manuscripts from the monasteries of the Levant; lovely corals from the Red Sea; dried herbs from China; chess-men carved in wood and ivory by Burmese prisoners. The visitors to his little shop were legion, though they were never men of title or importance. Lascars from the liners brought him precious stones and carvings picked up in the ports of the East; scholars and collectors in the humbler walks of life traded him ancient coins against gems or manuscripts. But no visitor ever escaped sharing a black coffee with him in the work-room at the back of the shop, and these business conversations enabled him to pick up a mass of miscellaneous information about foreign countries which was of the utmost interest to Dombey's little band of enthusiasts in SOq.

Boris was a Galician Jew who had emigrated to London in the early twenties and had rapidly established himself in business as a wig-maker; but his range of interests was too large to be confined, and he rapidly expanded his business in a hundred unorthodox directions. He had also in the past performed several difficult and dangerous missions for the organization to which Methuen belonged, though he never accepted a bounty for them. He would explain gravely that the security of British citizenship was a bounty freely bestowed upon him which he felt that he could never repay. To take money for his services to the Crown was more than he could bear. "What I do, I do because I am proud to be accepted in the British family," he would say, his hand on his heart.

Many had been the attempts to coax him into SOq, but he valued his independence too much to become a full member of an organization so exacting in its demands upon his time. He remained nevertheless an unofficial ally of the brotherhood, his usefulness growing with the years; he had become almost an institution, and there was hardly an operator who would undertake a mission to a little-known country without first asking Boris to offer him a brief. Methuen was no exception to the rule.

"Boris," he called again, and putting his ear to the flap of the letter-box was relieved to hear the familiar shuffling step of the wig-maker as he crossed the dark floor to the light-switch. The light came on and Boris stood there staring at him through the glass like a small and rather soiled penguin. His black beard was uncombed and he fumbled with the pince-nez which always dangled round his waist on a length of string. He got Methuen into focus at last and smiled. "Methuen!" he said. "Welcome back," drawing the stiff bolts of the door, and repeating "Welcome back". He locked the door carefully behind his visitor and led the way to the back of the shop. The great work-room was brightly lit, and full of the smell of coffee which simmered in a pot on the gas-stove.

Methuen looked around him with amused interest. "What have you got here?" he said. Boris rummaged in a cupboard for a cup and saucer. A large silver wig stood upon a wooden pedestal obviously half-finished; next to it, offering a grotesque contrast, were two shrunken human heads in bottles. "Peruvian," said Boris. "They came in yesterday. One is all that remains of Atahualpa, the Indian who started the revolution years ago, remember?" "My God," said Methuen, "one of these days someone is going to stroll in to you with my head in a bottle. You won't turn a hair."

Boris looked shocked. "I should be upsetted to see my friend in a bottle," he said severely. Sometimes he found it a little difficult to appreciate the English sense of humour. "I am selling these to the Science Museum," he added irrelevantly. "But my dear, my darling," he went on in a burst of enthusiasm, "wait till Dombey sees what I have for him." From a shelf he reached down two large cases of beautiful moths, neatly pinned to corks and classified. "Such beautiful things!"

They chatted for a while until the coffee-pouring ritual was at an end and they sat facing one another across the workbench. Then, idly fiddling with the little lapidary's wheel which stood near him, Methuen disclosed his plans. Boris put his hand to the side of his head and moved his face from side to side repeating "Aie! Aie!" very thoughtfully. "It is most difficult," he said. "I have good informations from a currency smuggler. Most difficult. The countryside is ruined. People starve. And you want to run around Serbia like a tourist with a fishing-rod."

Methuen felt rather slighted by this description of himself. "Not exactly a tourist," he said. "I want to know how I could live for a short while, say a week, in this territory which I know like the back of my hand."

"You must look like a Serb."

"What must I wear?"

"I will tell you."

As usual Boris's information was copious and exact. In a series of brilliant and exact strokes he built up a Serbian peasant: baggy woollen trousers tucked into heavy leather riding-boots; greasy fur cap; woollen cape. Methuen for his part wrote out a list of the equipment he intended to carry: a thermos, a pistol and ammunition, a solid fuel stove, matches, a trout-rod. ("He is mad," said Boris to the ceiling. "A trout-rod of all things!") But he could not help smiling. "I will find you", he said, "a three-quarter length duffle jacket and build you in poacher's pockets. Up here a pistol sling," he slapped his left collar-bone. "You will clink about like the men-at-arms in Drury Lane."

But already he was entering into the spirit of the thing. Money, for example, was little use. Communism had so de-

based currency that Methuen would be better advised to carry
a few needles and some pack-thread. He could always buy
eatables from the peasants with these. If he could fish without
getting caught he might live mostly on trout; but he must
beware of the police patrols. Nor could he count upon the
peasantry to help him, for they had been reduced to a state of
cowed subjection by the policy of collectivization and the police
terror. They would immediately disown an unknown man
living in their midst. "That is just it," said Metheun. "There
*are* only a few scattered villages in this area. It is all mountains,
Boris, completely cut off. I lived once for a month in a cave
there without seeing a soul."

Boris shook his head doubtfully. "It is a most difficult thing,"
he said. Nevertheless he set his mind wholeheartedly at Methuen's service, examining every aspect of the problem carefully
and in detail. Their conversation lasted long into the night and
when Methuen at last said good night and turned away down
the dark streets in the direction of his club he felt as if he had
just returned from a week spent in the mountains of Yugoslavia. Lying in bed in the dark he heard the ripple of the
torrents, still mushy with spring snow; saw the twinkle of
trout in the dark gulleys and fents of the Studenitsa river. And
fragment by fragment recaptured the details of those two lost
summers which he spent once with a Serbian friend, climbing
the dizzy escarpment near the Janko Stone, or swimming in
the black pools of water by the rocky river.

# CHAPTER THREE

## *Further Preparation*

I t was in one of these mountain-pools that he discovered the Mother and Father of Trout, an enormous and insolent brute, loitering among the shadows like a beadle in a church; he doubted if his slender line would take him, but as the shallows offered no impediment in the shape of rocks and reeds he thought that he might manage to play the beast until he tired of it. His fly dropped upon that black and polished surface like a kiss, and languidly the great trout rose to it. . . . Methuen woke to the rattle of his alarm-clock on the table by his bed. He yawned and sat up. It was ten o'clock and the grey sky foretold a day of drizzle which made the thought of Yugoslavia all the more inviting as a prospect. He shaved slowly while he waited for his breakfast, still mentally playing the great fish, letting him race to the end of the pool until he felt the nylon line stretched to breaking-point. . . . But there was an infinity of work and planning which stretched between him and that placid trout-stream in the hills.

With difficulty he addressed his mind to the tasks in hand. First he rang Dombey and said: "I'm on." Dombey pretended to show surprise. "I didn't think you would be," he said and laughed when Methuen swore at him. "You will proceed," he added, putting on a throaty accent, as of a duty clerk, "on the seventeenth instant by Orient Express. Travel department will have your papers by this afternoon. I have already sig-nalled Belgrade that you are going. You should see some of the signals I've got back in the last few days about the project."

"I'd like to," said Methuen grimly.

In fact he did, spending the morning quietly with the index files on Yugoslavia, studying the telegrams and despatches about the country composed by the little staff of specialists in the Chancery of the Belgrade Embassy there. He looked up Sir John Monmouth in the Foreign Office list and was dis-appointed to find nothing beyond the bare list of his appoint-ments; he was, however, mixing it up with *Who's Who* which raised his spirits somewhat by listing fishing among the more absorbing of the Ambassador's hobbies.

That afternoon he spent shopping at the Army and Navy Stores, filling out the little green invoice he had been given, and marking up his purchases to Foreign Office Special Orders Department. He treated himself to a new sleeping-bag, made of fine kapok-stuffed quilting, and a supply of fishing-line which he put on the same expense account. He was beginning to feel absurdly light-hearted. This feeling, he realized, would gradually disappear as he neared the theatre of operations. That evening he treated himself to a dinner at Scott's and a theatre, and when he reached his club surprised himself by staying up till past midnight reading a travel-book. He was normally an early bird. But soon these civilized pleasures would be out of his reach and he wanted to enjoy them to the full.

The following morning he walked in the grey bedrizzled streets, drinking in the smells of London, to the river. In the armoury at Millbank he presented his service order and was allowed to play about with pistols of every calibre and shape. Henslowe, the artificer, followed him about benevolently, showing him his wares with absurd pride. "You never turned in that Luger you borrowed, Colonel Methuen," he said re-proachfully. "I have to answer for it to the War Office." Methuen apologized. "It's lying in a swamp somewhere," he explained, and was immediately given an elaborate form to fill up with a description of how the weapon had been lost. "Just put L on D (lost on duty)," said Henslowe sorrowfully. "Now you say you want one with a silencer."

"Small," said Methuen. "Pocketable."

"There's a new point three eight," said Henslowe regretfully, but with the air of a haberdasher finding the right size of neck and wrist for a man of unusual shape. "Only for heaven's sake bring it back! You see," he added, "it's still on the experimental list. First time they've fitted a silencer of this pattern to a point three eight. It's a sweet weapon, werry sweet." He pronounced the word "weepon". He found the pistol in question and pressed it upon his visitor, holding it by the barrel. It was small but ugly looking. "The balance is not all it might be, sir. But it's a werry sweet weapon."

They tried it downstairs on the miniature range. "It'll do me very well," said Methuen. "I must say it hardly makes any noise at all."

"Just a large sniff, sir. Like a man with a cold."

"Send it up to me," said Methuen, and Henslowe inclined his head sorrowfully with the air of a man who is glad to serve, but who feels that he is in danger of losing a much-cherished possession. "You won't leave it in a swamp, will you, sir?" Methuen promised faithfully not to. "It's hard when we get so few nice things these days."

"I know."

On his way to the Shop he could not resist a last look round the Tate Gallery with its harvest of rippling canvases bathed in the cold grey light of a London sky.

Dombey was sitting in his office dictating from a sheaf of

papers into the mouthpiece of his dictaphone. "Come in," he said, switching off, as Methuen put his head round the door. "Come in and tell me all the news."

"Everything is in order. I came to give you an ultimatum: if I go to Yugoslavia I'm damn well going into the mountains to fish. If you want me to stay in Belgrade then the trip is off, and you can find someone else."

A crooked smile spread itself over Dombey's countenance. "My dear fellow," he said, "I should never stand in the way of a trouter. Never."

"Well, so long as that is understood."

"You are a free agent. If you think that you want to investigate the place where Peter met his death . . . who am I to say you nay?"

Methuen strode off down the corridor to the despatch-room and arranged for his parcel of effects to be delivered to the Foreign Office bag-room. They would be sent on to him under seal, while he himself was to travel in the character of the innocent Judson, the army accountant. That gave him an idea. He rang Dombey. "This man Judson," he said. "*Hist*," said Dombey. "Not on the phone. Come to my office." Methuen returned to find his chief glaring indignantly at a memo written in the round feminine hand of the Chief Secretary. "In the past seven days," he read out, "we have monitored all phone conversations in the SOq building. Out of a hundred conversations ten concerned confidential matters. *This must stop*." He sighed. "It is perfectly intolerable. We are back in the Middle Ages. We *have* to use the phone for something . . . what were you asking?"

"Judson," said Methuen. "What does he look like?"

"Like an accident. Adenoids. Spots. Flat feet. Constipation. Colds. Heavy underwear. Horn-rimmed spectacles."

"All right. All right."

"Passport section will give you all the information you need about him. They've fixed up his passport to fit you."

They had done more than this; they had obliged him with a Yugoslav ration card, an identity card, and a sheaf of points which would, all things being equal, enable him to purchase enough textiles for two shirts in Belgrade. It was quick work. Methuen retired to an empty office and put in a toll call to Ravenswood, the little country pub in which he spent all his holidays. Septimus answered almost at once with his great growling voice of welcome. "But of course, Colonel Methuen; of course we've room. Pity it's only for a night though—can't you make it longer?"

"I wish I could," said Methuen.

"Never mind," said Septimus. "I'll see that there's something worth eating for dinner. What time will you be in?"

"About seven-thirty."

"I'll send the pony trap."

"Don't worry. I'll walk through the fields."

Septimus groaned; nobody over eighteen stone can bear to hear the word "walk".

"I'd rather you than me," he said.

That night Methuen left the little station of Ravenswood and walked across the wet fields to The Parson's Nose, already preoccupied with the problems of his mission. Septimus and his buxom wife greeted and made much of him and he found that they had given him the best bedroom.

He spent a happy hour playing darts in the tap-room with his village acquaintances before confronting the kind of dinner for which Septimus was famous. Then he read for a while before turning in, full of an unhurried contentment. The book was *Walden* which he never tired of; a little India-paper edition which he always carried when he was out in the wilds and out of which he had evolved a laborious private code for keeping in touch with Dombey. Indeed he had first selected the book as a code-book, only to fall under its spell after many re-readings in solitary places.

He lay for a long time that night in the darkness, listening to the deep stillness of the English countryside and gathering himself together for the new mission which he knew would tax his resources to the utmost. Somewhere a nightingale sang softly, with a magical lazy clarity. The scent of honeysuckle came in at the open windows, and he could hear the soft whisper of rain in the leaves outside the window-sill. Ah! the familiar luxury of England! Why was one such a fool, to trade it against the chances of a nameless grave in an Asiatic swamp or on a Bosnian mountain?

For a wild moment he thought of ringing Dombey up and telling him: "I've changed my mind. I'm going on to the retired list for good. I'll stay right here in Ravenswood until I die." The longing was so great that he even rose on one elbow in the dark and reached out towards the telephone by his bed; but he knew in his heart of hearts that he would never lift the receiver off its hook. He must go on this new mission. Yet to assuage the thought of telephoning he got out of bed and rang up Boris. The wig-maker's voice sounded remote and crackly, and was half-submerged in a buzz of talk. "I have some friends here," he explained. "But your fancy dress is delivered this morning. I hope it fits you. *Sbogom*, my dear fellow."

"*Sbogom*," said Methuen and the word ("Go with God") took him back once more to those remote mountain fastnesses where the golden eagle brooded and where the deep swift rivers rushed between wooded banks on their way to the sea. Smiling, he fell asleep.

CHAPTER FOUR

# *The Journey Begins*

Lochon in the grey early morning looked unbelievably lovely. From the window of his loitering taxi Methuen let his eye rest briefly and lovingly on the familiar landmarks etched from the grey morning mist and felt once more the nostalgic tug of England which always afflicted him most when he was about to leave her. Passing St. James's Park he cried: "Stop a moment," and for a few minutes walked on the green grass beside the road. There was a heavy dew, even for early June, and as he stood looking around him Big Ben struck imperiously from the misty confines of the river.

When he reached Victoria he found he had some time in hand and swallowed a dreadful cup of tea in the buffet as he read an early morning edition. An item caught his eye for a moment among the general welter of type. "Yugoslav exiles to buy submarine." It was an item barely four lines in length which stated that the exiled Royalists in Paris had completed negotiations for the purchase of a submarine from Argentina. There did not seem to be any particular significance in it. A submarine would be of little use to an exiled government which owned neither Army or Navy. Did they blithely imagine that they were going to sail about the Mediterranean potting at Communist shipping in the Adriatic?

# The Journey Begins

He was extremely touched to find Dombey waiting for him at the barrier, looking more than ever like an owl and wrapped in a huge vague overcoat. "I wanted to see you off," he said. "I am really touched, Dombey," said Methuen. "I know what it must have cost you to get up as early as this." And he meant it.

He found his reserved seat and they walked up and down the platform for a while, arm in arm. "All your fancy dress is in the diplomatic bag," said Dombey. "I just wanted to see how much like an accountant you looked. Actually it is not bad." Methuen had dressed in a plain business-suit with a dark overcoat; his brief-case, umbrella, brown-paper parcel full of sandwiches proclaimed an inhabitant of the City of London. He had trimmed his moustache slightly and was wearing horn-rimmed spectacles which gave him a timid and urbane look. A pen and pencil were clipped into his vest pocket from which a neat triangle of handkerchief protruded.

"Why are they buying a submarine?" he asked.

"Heaven knows," said Dombey with the resignation of a man for whom the Balkan mentality is a closed book. "The thing is an old American one, stripped of all armament, and twice condemned. I doubt if one could take it to sea. It's been lying in a French dockyard under repair for ages."

A whistle blew and Methuen clambered aboard. "Look after yourself," said Dombey and Methuen told him not to fear anything on that score. The platform began to slide away with its coloured posters, for all the world as if a giant scene-shifter were at work. They ran out into the misty morning towards the grey Channel. Methuen felt his spirits rise as the train gathered way and the monotonous clicking of the wheels slithered and blurred into a rumble of speed.

Paris in the late afternoon was bright with sunlight, though there was hardly time to do more than glance at it. A blithe

## The Journey Begins

French taxi galloped Mr. Judson across the capital to the station where the Orient Express was lying, waiting for its passengers. Sunlight on the river and the animation of crowds which sauntered along its banks awoke many old memories. There were people he would have liked to see, but none of them were friends of Mr. Judson, so he forebore to telephone them. Mr. Judson was too timid to risk more than a glancing encounter with this capital of fun and good food—and so much vice. He found his *wagon-lit*, attended to his luggage, and disposed himself in gloomy silence to eat the bread and butter he had brought with him. Later, greatly daring, he bought a bottle of Vichy water, counting his change with a suspicious air, and waving away the proffered bottle of red wine which the man tried to press on him.

In the dining-car that night he was able to size up his fellow-passengers. There were two Italian families travelling part of the way, a few nondescript business men, and three surly-looking Yugoslavs obviously returning from some trade mission in western Europe. They talked all the time with animation but in low tones, while all their ordering was done by one member of the party who spoke a few words of French. They wore cheap overcoats of hideous cut and heavy boots, but seemed inordinately proud of the cheap wrist-watches they all wore on their right arms. Mr. Judson dined opposite them and while he could not hear the subject of their conversation he overheard enough to decide that they were all peasants who had found themselves elected officials under the new dispensation. Two at least were Serbian, while the one who spoke French was either a Croat or a Slovene.

At the Italian frontier they ran into heavy rain, and by the time the train reached Venice it had hardened into a storm which looked as if it might last for ever. A strong south wind whipped the shallow lagoons to a tawny yellowish froth and the clouds hung low over the city. Here there was a long wait. The train disgorged its passengers, and the polite and intelligent sleeping-car attendants packed their suitcases and took their leave. They were replaced by a couple of unshaven-looking rascals, smelling strongly of plum-brandy and dressed in soiled brown uniforms. Neither spoke any language but his own, and the few remaining passengers were reduced to express their wants in dumb-show. One small fragment of conversation gave Mr. Judson a valuable clue as to how one was expected to behave in Yugoslavia. One of the Yugoslavs aboard the train said, in the course of a long and unintelligible conversation: "I knew at once he was an anti-Titoist because he said '*Shogom*' instead of '*Zdravo*'." This puzzled Judson for a moment until he remembered that the first greeting carries the name of God with it, and to the good Marxist the name of God is anathema.

Darkness was falling as the train crawled into Trieste, and after a brief pause turned inland to climb the cliffs which separated them from the Yugoslavia which Methuen had once known so well but which Mr. Judson had never seen. At the frontier a horde of officials climbed aboard supervised by a couple of grim-looking young men in leather overcoats and top-boots, but dressed in plain clothes. Mr. Judson was interested in this first glance at the dreaded OZNA officials who held the country in a grip hardly less brutal than that of the Russian NKVD. They were obviously chosen for their powerful physique and not for their intelligence. They walked along the corridor holding the passports of the passengers and clumsily comparing the photographs which adorned these documents with the originals. They found that the likeness of Mr. Judson passed muster and handed him back his passport after taking the precaution of looking under the seats of the sleeping-carriage. The other officials treated them with great deference, and the swagger with which they walked proclaimed them a ruling caste. The diplomatic visa saved Mr. Judson from the indignity of having his baggage searched, though there was nothing incriminating in it.

Almost empty, the train passed the last barrier and lurched forward into the darkness which covered Yugoslavia. Methuen stared eagerly out of the window to pick up remembered landmarks but the darkness defeated him; once or twice he caught a glimpse of a fairy-tale mountain fringed with fir trees, rearing up against the sky, and perhaps dotted with Hans Andersen houses, with hanging eaves. Once or twice the darkness fell away under his eyes and showed him the racing whiteness of a mountain torrent, the steady concussion of the water rising above even the roar of the wheels. But for the most part the land lay in darkness except for where a blaze of light lit up a riverside sawmill or a power factory.

At Lunbliana the station was seething with human beings and almost before the train drew up a raging crowd of peasants burst into it, shouting incoherently and dragging after them shapeless parcels of all sizes.

There was no attempt to keep order, and so great was the press that even the corridors of the train filled to bursting point with human beings, who overflowed into the reserved sleeping-coaches and were expelled with oaths by the attendants. Methuen had a vivid memory of the pre-war Slovene peasant with his spotless linen and he was shocked to see the ragged and dirty crowd which now besieged the train. Everyone wore the shapeless cloth cap that was the badge of a new servitude. The women looked ghastly and haggard as they wrestled with their baskets, and the shrill voices with which they wrangled and argued had an edge of hysteria and fatigue. This was a new and startling phenomenon—the transformation of a Yugoslav crowd into a band of pariahs. Only the officials looked secure and well fed, each with his tall top-boots and black despatch case. The revolution had carried them to security above the common press of human beings.

The way to the lavatory was now effectively blocked and Methuen took a stroll to the end of the corridor, reserved for the privileged foreigners, to gaze at the bee-like swarm of passengers in the next carriage. Once the train started they seemed to relax into attitudes of fatigued sleep, some leaning, some standing. As he advanced into the corridor a large mustachioed peasant emerged from the lavatory and greeted him. He was an elderly man with a good expanse of dirty waistcoat and a moth-eaten fur hat. He was obviously rather drunk and carried in his right hand, with elaborate care, a bottle whose pungent odour proclaimed its contents—plum brandy. His broad humorous face proclaimed him a Serb. "Ah," he said, "a foreigner."

"Eh?" said Mr. Judson, peering at him.

"Well may you stare at us," said the Serb, describing an arc with his free hand. "Well may you see what they are doing to our country. Come, follow me." This was too good to miss; still smiling uncomprehendingly Mr. Judson allowed the heavy arm to propel him into the crowded corridor. Apparently the old farmer had his seat in the first carriage reserved for him. He sat himself down unsteadily after a good deal of clawing at the arms and shoulders of those who blocked the entry. "Here is a foreigner," he announced to the company at large. Rabbit-glances of uncertainty from all corners of the carriage greeted this statement. "I really must go," said Mr. Judson, who seemed too timid to disengage himself from the burly peasant's grasp. "He is seeing what they have done to our country," said the old man, who felt he had got hold of a point and wanted nothing better than to stick to it. "Our country," he added, taking a swig from the bottle.

"Let him go," said a timid-looking girl. "Don't bother him, he is a foreigner and doesn't understand."

The old man gave another grandiloquent flourish of his arm: "He will understand one day," he said. "When the white eagles come again. Now they are far, far." He raised his fingers to the ceiling and screwed up his eyes as if trying to spot a distant object in an empty sky. "But one day they will come." This little effort produced a quite extraordinary effect of alarm in the carriage. Three people, including a policeman, obviously returning from leave, immediately pretended to fall fast asleep and snore. A young soldier and two women got up hastily and left the carriage, after casting a frightened glance at each other. A man in plain clothes who had been reading a newspaper, dropped it. "Far, far," repeated the old man.

A tall young militiaman who had been standing in the corridor stuck his head in and shouted: "Enough of your nonsense or we shall put you off the train." He pushed the old man's arm off Judson's and stood back to let him pass, saying: "If you please," with great politeness. Reluctantly Mr. Judson relinquished his new-found acquaintance and made his way back to his own compartment. He decided to hunt out a book from his suitcase and discovered that it had been clumsily searched, no doubt in his absence. He ordered his bed to be made up and settled himself to read. Whatever else happened, he reflected, nobody could deny that this was going to be a most interesting journey.

They did not reach Zagreb until after midnight, and here once more a sleepy Methuen stared out upon a platform seething with ragged serfs. Huge socialist-realist posters stabbed the ill-lit gloom with their invocations to the God of Marxist progress. Everywhere too were slogans written in dazzling capitals on the walls, and picture upon picture of Tito, flanked by Stalin and Lenin, or flanked by members of his own inner cabinet, the Politburo. The contrast between the promises held out by those flaring posters and the bitter reality of life under Communism seemed fantastic to the sleepy watcher at the window. It was as if he were entering a new country, so little did these scenes correspond to his own memories of a joyous, confused but essentially happy country. To be sure the trains and stations had been crowded before; to be sure people had been rather careful what they said in front of the police; but what had changed now was not the situation so much as the human being. These ragged creatures seemed to have lost all self-respect in the struggle to make ends meet. They had become submerged in the rising tide of an anonymous, faceless, characterless mass. It was rather frightening. And everywhere, walking with authority and arrogance, he saw the officials of the ruling caste—either blue-clad militia or the ubiquitous gentlemen in leather overcoats whose function was to hold the ring for the Communist party.

He slept now, and in his dreams saw the great plains unrolling like a chart on either side of the train, traversed by dense swift rivers. The train gathered speed and clanked onwards towards Belgrade, occasionally emitting a drowsy shriek, or spewing forth a handful of burning clinkers which set fire to the dry sedges beside the railway. The monotonous lulling chant of the wheels took possession of him and he did not wake until he heard the roar of the train passing over the last bridge which spans the Sava river and leads directly into the heart of the capital.

He was met at the station by a junior accountant, a spotty and respectful young man who obviously had no clue that the identity of the Mr. Judson he was expecting was being used as a mask. Methuen thought it wiser not to enlighten him. He loaded his luggage into the car and sitting beside the young man, jogged and sprawled his way up towards the Embassy.

"Major Carter is going to put you up in his villa, sir," said the young man, not without a touch of envy. "Better than the hotels here."

"I hear," said Methuen, "that you have lost your M.A."

The young man lowered both his head and his voice. "It's been a great shock, sir. We've just sent the body back to London, sir. A great shock. And you know, sir, they say he wasn't only shot; he looked as if he had been crushed. All bruised."

Methuen said nothing for a moment, watching the shabby battered streets of the capital flicker past outside the windows of the car. "He may have had a bad fall," he said. "He used to go off on fishing trips, didn't he?"

The young man put on an arch and knowing air. "If you ask me," he said, "he was up to something else. However," he went on, pursing his lips, "it is none of our business. It's not our side of the work. We must mind our own business." Methuen agreed gravely and let the matter rest.

The car rambled out towards the wooded residential area of the town and after exploring a number of leafy and ill-paved roads stopped before a villa on the balcony of which sat a young fair-headed man taking his breakfast. "That's the Major," said Methuen's companion as the young man rose from the table and came out to the gate.

"I'm Judson," said Methuen, shaking hands.

"I know," said Carter with a twinkle in his eye as he led the way across the garden to the terrace where breakfast for two had been laid. "We've had a series of signals about your coming to inspect the accounts. Will you breakfast first or have a bath?"

Methuen chose to have a bath and a shave. While he was unpacking his suitcase Carter came and sat on a chair in his room. "Can one talk freely here?" asked Methuen. The young man nodded. "Servants are at the other end of the house. There's a microphone in the drawing-room down which I sometimes shout obscenities, but this place is not wired for sound."

"I gather," said Methuen, shaving, "that a distinctly chilly reception awaits me. I saw all the telegrams from the Ambassador."

"Yes. He was dead against your coming. Afraid of creating further trouble. And frankly I myself wondered what the point was unless of course. . . . But you would be mad to try and explore the territory that Peter broke into. It's probably alive with police. I wanted to go but was refused permission."

"You see," said Methuen, "SOq thought I might be of use as I know that stretch of mountains awfully well indeed; and I can speak the language quite well."

"So did Peter."

"I know."

"Have they discovered that he was using the duty run to Skoplje as a ferry?"

"I don't know. There's a place in the road where the police car drops behind owing to the dust. Sometimes as much as a quarter of a mile. Plenty of time to slow down and drop somebody off. As a matter of fact Peter made a habit of dropping off duty cars on their consular runs. He explored the area around Nish—we have a consulate there too, in the same way."

"He was lucky to get away with it."

"It was risky certainly; but you see we were working to find out something about the Royalist underground. I suppose you've seen the detailed summaries of all the arrests, and the lists of equipment which they claim to have taken."

"What can be behind it?"

"Come and have some breakfast. We can talk about it when you've made your number with the Ambassador."

"If and when," agreed Methuen.

They walked out on to the sunny terrace to take their breakfast.

## CHAPTER FIVE

# *The Ambassador Doubts*

"The Ambassador doubts very much—he very much doubts whether you will be of any use to the Mission," said the portly first secretary, joining the tips of his fingers together and pouting. "Nevertheless he has asked to see you. I feel I must warn you, however, that he very much doubts."

"Yes. Yes," said Methuen mildly. "I understand."

The first secretary pressed a bell and lifted his desk-telephone. "Marriot here, sir," he said. The receiver cracked shrilly. "I would like to bring Mr. Judson up to you."

In silence they walked across the large carpeted Chancery where the six young secretaries bent to their work in silence, across a dismal looking hall-way, to the lift. As they began the slow ascent the first secretary hummed a little tune under his breath. He led the way down a series of well-lit corridors lined with hunting scenes and into a magnificent room where the Ambassador stood in an attitude of deep dejection before a rippling log fire.

"Colonel Methuen, sir," said the secretary, retreating and shutting the door on his charge.

"Come in," said the Ambassador.

"Good morning," said Methuen.

43

# The Ambassador Doubts

There was a long and chilly silence. Sir John was a tall and graceful figure of a man, in his early sixties, and with a fine head of silver hair which he wore closely cropped. He was dressed in a black coat and striped trousers with a collar of old-fashioned cut. He regarded Methuen for a while in silence with an absent-minded air before asking him to sit down and offering him a cigarette which he lit for him. "Colonel Methuen," he said quietly, "I know the work of your people and admire it very much." It was an unexpected compliment but none the less pleasing for a soldier. "I don't doubt you've seen my telegrams," went on Sir John in the same quiet tone, and Methuen admitted that he had. "I must say, sir," he said, "I fully appreciate the delicacy and difficulty of your mission here; and I sincerely hope that you won't find me any trouble to you."

Sir John sat down and sighed, and Methuen could see his face become suddenly tired and old-looking. "Peter Anson is a great loss to us," said the old man, joining his hands together. "I can't disguise the fact. He was not only charming and intelligent. He was a first-class officer. But he had no business to exceed his brief by exploring the country illegally. The mere fact of a man attached to a diplomatic mission doing that brings discredit on us. It makes our work infinitely harder, it ruins confidence in us. You will understand that."

"I do, sir," said Methuen.

"I am anxious that you should not add to the burden by doing the same thing. You may think it a selfish view. You see our work is based on confidence. It is not done in a day but over a period of years. One incident like this can destroy confidence which has taken us a year or more to build up. Now Dombey seems to think——"

"As a matter of fact, sir," said Methuen, "Dombey ordered me to stay here in Belgrade. It was my own idea to follow

Anson to try and discover how he met his death. I know the area well. And as a matter of fact, quite apart from anything else, I was hoping to fish a river I knew many years ago."

"Fishing?" the Ambassador pricked up his ears. "My dear chap, how on earth can you hope——?"

"I was proposing to go native for a week or so and explore the mountains where Anson went to fish. There are three or four small rivers there packed with trout. I know it sounds silly."

A new and purposeful gleam lit the Ambassador's tired eyes as he heard this. "Fishing," he said, under his breath, and Methuen saw a smile beginning to dawn in his eyes. "You solemnly intend to go fishing?" He patted the blotter on his desk with a white hand and his eyes twinkled.

"After all, sir, I gather Anson managed a few illicit week-ends. It should not be impossible. The mountains hereabouts used to be quite deserted. They can't have changed so very much."

"I must say," said Sir John, and a note of envy crept into his voice, "it is maddening to live here and be unable to fish. This limitation on our movements is galling. I fish myself, you know."

"Splendid. Then perhaps you won't think my idea quite mad. You see," Methuen went on in a burst of confidence, "I think I could easily pass as a Serb at a pinch, and I wouldn't really feel more out of place in this area than you would in your home county in England. The whole thing has been most carefully considered, sir—the mission, not the fishing—and it is nowhere near as foolhardy as it sounds."

"I see," said Sir John, and thought profoundly for a moment. Then he got up abruptly and walked over to the great wall-map hanging behind his desk. "Where exactly would you go if I gave you permission to?" Smiling, Methuen followed him and with a brown finger touched the mountain range in question. "Exactly," said the Ambassador triumphantly. "So would I. These tributaries up here for example. They——"

"The rivers form great pools here——"

"What tackle have you?"

The reader must be spared the details of a conversation which now lasted for nearly an hour and a half, between two enthusiasts of the rod. Sir John was a bachelor and fishing for him was almost a religion: at any rate Methuen found that *Who's Who* had been guilty of an error in describing his passion for the sport as a "hobby". It was a good deal more than that. Together they explored almost every lake and river in Yugoslavia, crossing and recrossing the great wall-map to dwell, now upon the merits of the great trout of the Vrba river, now upon the difficulties of fishing some of the Slovene rivers. The old man listened with the greatest eagerness and delight to Methuen's exposition of the fishing conditions in the country. "I shall put all this to good use one day," said Sir John. "You say the Olive Dun is not much of a draw? I should have thought in the muddier ones, at the late springtime when the snow melts——"

"Not in my experience," said Methuen who had lost his nervousness of this august figure by now and was delighted to find a fellow fisherman. The Ambassador now unlocked a compartment of his desk and took from it a book of flies whose beauty and ingenuity made Methuen envious. Some of these he had made himself, and he drank in Methuen's enthusiastic praise with the delight of a schoolboy. The conversation now reverted to cases, and Methuen told his story of the fourteen-pounder which he had lost after a long battle on a tributary of the Spey. The Ambassador capped this with an experience of his own. Types of rod were discussed. The Ambassador rang for coffee, and over it they expanded their range to cover nearly the whole field of fishing.

## The Ambassador Doubts

"My goodness," said Sir John, "*how* I regret this silly ban on travel. Methuen, if I let you go on this trip you must promise me to be careful. It's not only the danger that worries me. I don't want the authorities to have another excuse to protest to H.M.G. And yet: the whole thing is so foolhardy I shouldn't really countenance it."

"Well, the decision is yours, sir," said Methuen.

The Ambassador walked up and down the room for a moment with his hands behind his back. "It isn't really," he said, and there was a touch of sadness in his voice. "I've been overruled by the F.S. I can't disguise from you the fact that his decision is extremely galling. We Ambassadors are paramount chiefs in our territories. But I suppose that special considerations were at stake. Your personal safety is the Awkward Shop's affair, of course. But I'd like you to give me your word, as an officer and a fisherman," he smiled slowly, "that you will bear my preoccupations in mind, and won't cause us any trouble on the diplomatic front."

"Of course I will," said Methuen.

Sir John pressed a bell and asked for a telephone number. "Carter," he said, "come up and see me, please." He added as an aside: "My dear Colonel, I am beginning to envy you," but then some afterthought of the dangers and hazards of the trip must have crossed his mind for he shook his head and frowned. There was a tap at the door and Carter came in.

"Ah, Carter. I'm afraid Colonel Methuen has talked me into his scheme. It sounds a good deal more reasonable than it did at the beginning. I've changed my mind. He is going to follow Anson. Will you arrange the details for him and see that there are no slip-ups?"

"Yes, sir," said Carter with a certain obvious astonishment. "I certainly will."

47

"I can't thank you enough, sir," said Methuen, "and believe me I shall try not to cause any trouble."

Sir John shook hands with warmth. "When you come back," he said, "we must spend an evening together. It gets rather lonely, you know. I've no one on my staff who fishes. And by the way, if you would care to . . . I'd be honoured, Colonel. . ." and with a gesture which was almost shy he placed his cherished book of flies in Methuen's hands.

In the corridor outside Methuen could not resist a chuckle at Carter's look of blank amazement. "Is it really on?" said the young soldier with excitement. "What on earth have you done to His Excellency? He was dead against the trip when Dombey hinted at it." Methuen sighed, and as they stepped into the lift he said: "He's a fisherman." Carter grinned. "I see." Then he went on more seriously. "Frankly you know the assignment is a risky one. I'm not altogether convinced of your wisdom in going, sir. And I do hope that you won't take it too lightly." Methuen smiled at him. "Because I am taking a trout-rod?" he said. He was turning the book of flies over in his fingers, mentally selecting those which he thought might suit his purpose. Carter added once more, as if alarmed by these signs of abstraction, "I hope you won't take it too lightly."

"No," said Methuen thoughtfully. "You need not worry on that score. I don't make an uninsurable occupation more dangerous than it is by taking it lightly."

Carter's office was a long pleasant room with a certain austere bareness, due perhaps to the unpolished trestle tables which lined one wall. Here a huge sectional map of the country was laid out in pages. A celluloid grid and a magnifying-glass lay on it. Carter cleared his throat and sat down after fetching his guest a chair. "I expect you know as much as I do, sir," he said. "Peter bunged himself off in the car with a light bed-roll, a fishing-rod, and a couple of tins of Spam. He was fully dressed when they brought him in; shot through the head at point-blank range. But he was also very badly bruised, perhaps from a fall. Oh! one or two other small items of gear have not yet reappeared: glasses, an oil compass. Frankly, anyone would pinch them off a body. But what is curious is that the only book he took with him was still in the pocket of his coat. Here it is." He took a small volume of Serbian folk-songs out of his desk and passed it to Methuen. "He picked it up second-hand. As you will see from the names in the front it has been used by several schoolboys who are most probably responsible for the marginal comments."

Methuen turned the ugly little book over in his hands. "Go on," he said.

"Funny thing," said Carter. "Probably has nothing to do with the case, but I found one passage which looked as if it might have been marked by Peter. Let me show you." But he could not find it immediately. "It's about white eagles. Now there is something else which is baffling. Peter did tell me that he was making some progress, and that he had discovered an underground Royalist opposition which called itself Society of the White Eagles. You know of course that the white eagle is the old Serbian Royalist emblem. But he wouldn't tell me anything or write anything down until he had it all cleared up."

"White eagles," said Methuen reflectively. "May I keep this book awhile? I suppose you have no clue as to where he slept? Did he mention a cave? There is a network of caves along the gorges of the Studenitsa river which would make an excellent hide-out."

"No. I gathered he slept in a forest. There were pine-needles stuck in his clothes. His wallet with some money and a few flies was also in his clothes when they brought him in."

"Anything else that struck you?"

"Nothing at all. For once I think the authorities are telling

the truth. I think they did find him. As to who shot him up—
it's anyone's guess. He was unarmed."

Methuen ruffled the pages of the little Serbian book and
stared at the carpet for a moment, lost in thought.

"When is the next bag?" he said at last.

"This afternoon."

"And when is the next duty run through this area?"

"Day after to-morrow. You'd better meet Porson, he is in
charge of the bag and usually drives it down with him. I'll ring
the Chancery."

Porson proved to be a lanky and extremely youthful secretary, whose tousled head suggested that he had spent all
morning grappling bodily with matters of state. In fact, as sixth
secretary he had spent an hour trying to make a *placement* for
his Ambassador's dinner-party. It had been a baffling and exhausting task, and he had finally been driven to the end of en-
durance. He had been trying to accommodate twelve couples
round the Embassy dining-table in such a way as to give each
person the seat most appropriate to his or her rank. It was a
very burdensome problem: but then, he reflected, to be the
junior secretary among six inevitably meant that he had the
chores to deal with. There was however one great compensa-
tion for his lowly rank. It was he who was allowed to drive the
courier down to Skoplje every week—a journey which virtually gave him three days' leave in every seven. Although he
was disposed to complain about the trials of his post, nothing
would have induced him to surrender the one real privilege
which went with it. Despite the air of diffidence with which he
greeted Methuen now the latter decided that there was a
becoming touch of irreverence about the young man which
would make him an amusing companion. "I've read about you,
sir," he said.

"Methuen," said Methuen.

"Colonel Methuen," amended Porson, putting his monocle in his eye and gazing innocently around him. "I must say," he said, "from the telegrams I thought that the Ambassador would never agree to your mission."

"I know. But he has now."

"And you want to do exactly what Anson did?" Porson sighed. "Well, I wish you luck."

Methuen smiled and thanked him. "A few days in the mountains might teach us something," he said. "When do you go?"

Porson explained carefully. "We start from here every Wednesday and reach the Ibar valley by about four. There is a white milestone by the road which is the point of rendezvous. There's a deep ditch into which you will have to hurl yourself. At least that's what Anson did. We make the return run on Saturday night, reaching the same point of rendezvous at about dawn on Sunday morning. We get back here about ten usually."

"That's excellent," said Methuen, "but the time is rather short. That only gives me Thursday and Friday actually free to explore. I should like to stay a whole week if possible and walk around a bit."

"Well," said Porson, "come down on Wednesday and back Saturday week." Methuen nodded and agreed. "That would be perfect. Meanwhile, of course, if I run into trouble and need to get out you will be passing the rendezvous point twice, won't you, going back and forward? Is there any way I can get a message back to you, for example, even if I don't want to return myself?"

"Yes," said Porson. "We never used this method but Anson thought it out. About fifty yards beyond the milestone in question there is an enormous fig tree which overhangs the road. If you were to drop anything out of it we could easily field it as we went past. At least that's what Anson thought."

"Splendid," said Methuen, "so that I shall feel that I am in touch with you all the time. You see, suppose I discover some-thing which is of importance but which makes it necessary to wander a good way into the mountains, I could let you know. Alternatively if I needed anything you could drop it for me in the same ditch."

They discussed the various possibilities of the scheme in detail. Porson scratched his chin and said: "It sounds to me as if you intend to stay up there for weeks. I do hope someone has told you how dangerous cross-country travel is in this country. Anson, you know, was not foolhardy. He was a most cautious character."

Methuen stubbed out his cigarette. "I am going to be doubly cautious," he said. "And anyway once Anson was caught he could not pose as a Serb. I can, and that might be some help. Of course all this is only speculation."

"Well," said Porson, "I must say I admire your nerve. I don't think I should be able to do it with such jolly old sang-froid. Have you told Dombey that the trip is on?"

"No. Perhaps I'd better."

Porson led the way to the Chancery where Methuen drafted a telegram telling Dombey of his intentions. "I think," he said, "we should send this as we are starting. In case Dombey suddenly gets cold feet and holds me up."

"As you wish," said Porson. "As you wish, dear old fire-eating Colonel."

Meanwhile some attempt was being made to help Methuen create the character of Mr. Judson, for the benefit of the other inhabitants of the building. He was given a small office of his own with a desk and an immaculate blotter, and the account books of the Military Attaché's office were stacked up before him. He ruffled the pages of figures in some perplexity before putting them on one side. The sanctuary was useful, however, for it enabled him to study once more the mass of documentation which had grown up around the spy-trials. He re-read the newspaper accounts of the trials, making careful notes of anything which might have a bearing on his mission, and following each stage of the inquiry on the excellent map that Carter put at his disposal. It was certainly difficult to imagine why there should be persistent infiltration of armed agents into precisely this area; first of all, any activity here could be easily contained by troops and police. While the barren mountain-range offered fair chances of protection against discovery it would be a hopeless project to attempt to start up a revolution against Tito here. The one railway which crossed this area was not only difficult to cut, since it ran through a series of rock-tunnels cut high in the cliff-face of the gorge, but potential wreckers would have to cross the wide and extremely swift Ibar river to reach it. Even if one could form and maintain a strong guerilla band on the mountains behind the Studenitsa Gorge there would be little point, for there were no targets in this area worth their attention. The towns were few and of little strategic importance. The more he pondered over it the more confusing the problem became.

He turned to the little Serbian collection of folk-songs which Anson had carried with him and went through it carefully. There was one passage underlined which seemed to him the one that Carter had been hunting for.

> *In his extremity the king will go*
> *To the mother and father of rivers,*
> *Where the sources meet*
> *And the white eagles fly in families,*
> *To find his patrimony here*
> *Buried in the ground.*

This seemed to offer little contribution to the argument; doubtless Anson had marked it for its beauty rather than for any hidden significance. Nevertheless he memorized the pass-age before putting the book on one side. In the cipher-room he concocted a long signal to Dombey explaining his intentions, and giving a brief outline of the latest evidence (since he left London a further group of armed "bandits" had been cap-tured operating in the same area). Then he went out for a walk through the shabby streets of the capital he had once known so well.

# CHAPTER SIX

## *Further Perplexities*

Carter took him to lunch that day, and afterwards they drove out along the loops of the Sava river with its melancholy avenues of giant willows, talking in desultory fashion about their project. Porson came with them and enlivened the afternoon with his ribaldries, and his accounts of the trials and tribulations of secretaries. By tea-time the bag arrived and Methuen claimed the large cardboard box which contained his fancy dress. There was a note attached to it from Boris which read: "Herewith your cloak of invisibility. Hope you don't clank." He carried off this prize to the privacy of Carter's villa and after locking himself in the bedroom tried out his disguise. "Gosh," said Carter hovering between admiration and laughter as he saw the progressive stages of Mr. Judson's transformation. "What do you think?" said Methuen with a touch of self-consciousness. He turned away from the mirror and faced his companion. On his head he wore a stained and moth-eaten fur cap of an unmistakably Serbian cast. His feet were clad in patched riding-boots with the traditional concertina-like frill at the ankles. A dirty shirt and waistcoat and a woollen scarf offset a pair of nondescript breeches cut vaguely after the fashion of jodhpurs. "But this," he said, spreading the wings of his coat, "this is the masterpiece." Boris had taken an old blue seaman's jacket made in heavy duffle. Inside he had fixed two great poacher's pockets as well as a pistol sling. Together with the inside and outside pockets it would be possible to carry all his small gear on his back. "Clank I probably will," said Methuen to himself, "but this will help me to move house in a hurry if I need."

"It really is very good," said Carter with envy. "Only you can't start from here looking so darned bucolic. You'll have to change in the car. There'll be plenty of room actually."

"So be it," said Methuen, starting to resume his formal black chartered accountant's uniform. The cardboard box was carefully locked away in Carter's safe against the journey, and Mr. Judson returned to the Embassy to wrestle with the accounts. In fact he spent an exhausting hour with Porson going over the whole journey in detail, and most particularly with that part of it which concerned him most. He was glad that there was a short breathing spell before he undertook the next and most hazardous part of the adventure. He liked to feel his way into the part he was to play, and to let all the available evidence fall into a pattern in his mind.

Having prepared himself as well as he reasonably could for the hazards of the trip he asked Carter to take him out to dinner, and if possible to the opera. He wanted to make a complete break with the subject of his preoccupation: to let it simmer on in the subconscious while he was left free to be, for however short a time, a normal man, enjoying everyday things. But the mind is a capricious thing. Once started along a train of reasoning it is not easy to sidetrack it with lighter distractions; moreover the mind itself, when busy with a problem, is often like a hound on the scent. Without any conscious effort it leads one further and further along the road of inquiry, picking up evidence.

How else can one account for the fact that Methuen, finding

he had an hour to spare before the Embassy closed, strolled into the central registry and asked for the master-file containing the despatches written during the last few months. He was simply amusing himself and collecting a little political background material. But idly reading through the despatches, his attention was drawn to one which described the nature and contents of radio broadcasts from Belgrade. After summarizing the various types of programme the report referred to the "apparently endless series of national poems which are broadcast one at a time, after the eight o'clock news every evening by the famous actress Sophia Maric". Something in the back of his mind told him that there was a clue to be discovered behind this simple observation and it was with a pleasant sense of anticipation that he turned to the files of the BBC monitoring station—that prodigious organization which records almost every radio programme in the world. It was not difficult to turn up the broadcasts in question. The titles of the poems read were neatly listed and Methuen saw, with some emotion, that the little poem, part of which has already been quoted, was the first to be broadcast, and was repeated twice during the first week.

He took this fragment of information along to Carter, who refused to be excited by it. "It is most likely just a coincidence. After all, every schoolboy is given a pretty steady diet of these damned epics and folk-songs. I listen to these recitations you know: my Serbian teacher makes me do it as pronunciation practice. In fact I'm working from the very book that Sophia Maric is reading from; I remember noticing that she is using *The National Treasury* because she gives the number of each poem at the beginning and end of the transmission."

"Could I see your copy?"

Carter obligingly ferreted it out from among a stack of papers and Methuen retired once more to the central registry and reopened the monitoring files. The broadcasts had begun about three months previously—in fact just about the time that reports of the first arrests of Royalist "bandits" had begun to be published. If only he could trace the smallest connection between one thing and the other. . . . Methuen sighed deeply and shook his head as he read through the highly coloured romances of feudal times. What a jumble of Slav imagery to wander through! How could there be any kind of message embedded in all this? Nevertheless he noticed one thing of interest. Several of the poems had been repeated twice by the actress. "Suppose," he said to himself, "there was some kind of message to be passed. Repeating a poem might draw attention to it. The listener would know that a twice-repeated poem was one containing a message."

This was all very well; but the poems themselves offered very little foothold for his theory. He was putting away his files when Carter and Porson came down with their red despatch-cases and found him waiting there. "Closing time," said Porson. "Away with dull care. Carter and I are going to take you out to dinner, old man. You will be allowed to choose it of course."

"Did you have any luck?" said Carter.

"None at all."

"Bad luck. I thought there was nothing in it."

"Nevertheless I'll take your book home if you don't mind and re-read the poems I've marked as having been twice recited."

But he was not happy at dinner; his mind was tugging at the problem as if it were on a leash. A curious kind of sixth sense told him that there was something to be made of this jumble of words if only he could find the key.

They dined in one of the only three eating-places available to foreigners: for almost every restaurant in Belgrade had been turned into a canteen where the ragged and half-starved proletariat queued up for its ration of ill-cooked food. Around them in the gloomy ill-lit Majestic Hotel sat the sleek and shaven members of the police and the party, and the fat sleepy members of the intelligentsia—the artists and writers who had given in. An air of desperate, shiftless boredom reigned over everything. Porson made one or two desperate sallies, which fell flat upon the stale air of the place. Then he too fell silent. "I hope," said Methuen, "that I am not depressing you. The truth is those damned folk-songs and epics are still going round and round in my mind. I feel there's something very obvious which I have missed there." Carter smiled and shook his head: "False scent," he said. "I bet you a fiver."

"My concern," said Porson, "is gastronomic. This omelette tastes like Stalin's moustache."

They walked out into the main square of the town together and Methuen smelt the curious stale smell that the Yugoslav public seemed to carry everywhere with them: sour sunflower-oil and rancid *kaimak*. It hurt him to see how shabby and frightened everyone looked. He had heard of police terror but this was the first time he had come across anything which permeated the very air of the town. The silence, too, was extraordinary; nobody sang or talked aloud, there were no shouts or whistling. Only the dull clump of boots on the broken and scarred pavements of the town. The scattered street lamps carved great pools of black shadow under the trees. At the door of the opera a crowd seethed, waiting to buy rejected tickets. They made a way for the foreigners and looked at them with a hang-dog air of sheepish envy. At the same time two large sleek limousines drew up at the door and the chauffeurs raced to open the car doors for a small group of high party officials. At once there came a burst of sycophantic clapping which echoed in the hollow street like a burst of machine-gun fire.

# Further Perplexities

The performance of *Fidelio* was preceded by a speech about its dialectical significance by a young man with wavy hair who spoke with a strong provincial accent. He was very nervous and gabbled out his speech from a typescript. It consisted of a rigmarole about Marxist values and the meaning of art for the people. The audience waited in painful silence for it to end, and Methuen, watching the rows and rows of haggard faces from the box which had been placed at the Embassy's disposal, felt once more a stirring of pity for the boisterous, good-natured lackadaisical Serbs he had once known. There were a number of smartly dressed officers in the stalls, but what was so striking was the shabbiness of the women. Their clothes looked like the hastily improvised remnants of a jumble sale; they wore no make-up, and there was hardly a head of waved hair. For the most part they wore their hair brushed stiffly back and pinned with a cheap bone slide. "There it is," said Porson in a whisper, "drink it all in."

"I am," said Methuen grimly.

The young man on the stage spluttered to the end of his speech and stood aside; the lights began to tremble down. At this moment a spark of recognition flickered in a pair of dark eyes and Methuen sat up. There was a face he knew. For a moment he could not remember where he had met Vida—all he could remember was her name. And then, as he held her eyes with his and answered her look of recognition he remembered. In Bari at the end of the war she had served on his staff as an interpreter. Her father had been a noted Royalist diplomat and had died abroad. Vida had been brought up in France and had served in the Free French Forces throughout the war. She had been loaned to Methuen, and he had been most concerned to hear that she had returned to Yugoslavia after the liberation. Yet here she was, large as life, sitting with a half-smile of recognition on her face, not ten feet from him.

## Further Perplexities

He turned and whispered to Porson: "I think I see someone I know. Will you lend me your mackintosh and beret at the first interval? I might get a chance to speak to her." Porson seemed rather startled but he agreed breathlessly. He could not resist adding: "For God's sake be careful. She may be working for OZNA, you know." But Methuen had already thought of that. Yet from what he knew of the old Vida, the serious dark-haired child of royalist Serbia, he was sure of one thing: she would not give him away.

She seemed to be alone as she spoke to no one, and from time to time, even in the velvety half-light, Methuen could feel her eyes resting upon him. As the lights went up for the interval he stared hard at her and then rose; in the shadowy space at the back of the box he struggled into Porson's mackintosh, and once he was in the corridor he put on the old grey beret which appeared to be the sixth secretary's favourite defence against the rain. It was not ineffective as a disguise, for the mackintosh was old and shabby and hid his neat dark suit. Certainly he was not conspicuous in the shabby crowd which had already filled the foyer with the fumes of acrid cigarette-smoke. He shuffled across the marble floor and took up a position against a pillar, studying some notices of forthcoming productions. He did not as yet know whether Vida would come, and he was quite startled to feel the touch of her hand on his arm and hear her say in a low voice: "Zdravo, Comrade." He greeted her without turning round, and together they stood examining the notices intently. At their backs stood a small group of students debating something with tolerable loudness; conversation was possible though he could feel from Vida's tone of voice how afraid she was.

"I need your help," said Methuen in a low urgent voice. "What have you been doing since last we met?"

"Everything," she replied. "Now I am working for *them*,

61

for the OZNA. My family is in a concentration camp." He glanced sideways and saw once more that proud dark face with its cleanly cut nose and mouth. There are people whose basic truthfulness shines out of their eyes, and looking into hers, Methuen knew that she had not changed. "My dear," he said, "can't you get out?" She shook her head. "But I am working for *us* too," she added in a passionate whisper. "We must try and overturn this unjust system. Methuen, do they know in England?" A heavily built officer came up and stood beside Methuen to study the notices, shouldering them both aside to do so.

"No," he whispered.

"Our people admired and loved England. They cannot believe that England is helping these Communists."

Her eyes flashed and her hands clenched. For a moment Methuen feared she might burst out into a violent denunciation of the régime. He took her hand and pressed it. "The white eagles?" he said, and at the words an extraordinary change came over her.

"You know about us?"

"A little."

"Can you help us in England? Please, tell all who care for liberty and decency. Please help our cause." It was the old passionate Vida kindling behind the mask of a prematurely aged woman. "Tell me about yourselves," said Methuen. "We don't know enough about you. You distrust us."

"I know. And with cause! Did you not put our friend into power here?" She nodded towards a portrait of Tito on the foyer wall. A bell rang sourly and people began to stub out their cigarettes before drifting back into the auditorium. "I must go," she said, "I must go." "Wait," he said, "I must talk to you. Can we meet?" Her eyes darkened with fear and she hesitated. "Please," he said, "I may help you." She thought for a moment, a prey to confused emotions. Then at last her proud little face hardened again and she said: "To-morrow at the picture gallery in the Kalemigdan, the Turkish fort. Twelve. No greetings, please."

She slipped through the doors and was gone. Methuen went back to the box, a prey to conflicting emotions of triumph and uncertainty. If she were working for the OZNA she might report him and cause him trouble. On the other hand if she were really the Vida who had worked with him for two years he could be tolerably sure that she would not give him away— especially if she were really a member of the White Eagles! Meeting her might turn out to have been a stroke of real luck.

Throughout the rest of the performance he was restless, and unable to concentrate on the music, which pursued its listless course in the semi-darkness like a shallow but noisy river. Long before the end of the last scene he felt he had had enough and, obtaining the consent of his hosts, rose to leave; nor were Porson and Carter sorry to accompany him, for both were eager to hear if his rendezvous had been a success or not. They walked back through the ill-lit streets to the hotel where Porson's car was parked while he gave them an account of the meeting, and of his plans for the morrow.

"I must say it's a stroke of luck," said Carter, "if you feel you can trust her not to give you away."

"At any rate if I am starting the day after to-morrow I shall not be in evidence here. The OZNA would have to trace me before it can have me followed. Incidentally is one followed here?"

Porson groaned. "Of course."

"Not inside the theatre."

"No. But there was a leather man waiting outside for us."

"I'm getting unobservant," said Methuen.

"Cars are only followed if they cross a check point on the three roads outside Belgrade unattended by an OZNA car."

"I shall have to drop off in town somewhere," said Methuen, "for the meeting to-morrow."

They returned to Porson's flat and over a drink discussed the problem anew before they went their ways to bed.

"I think the omens are good," said the lanky young diplomat with a solemnity and deliberation much heightened by the whisky he had drunk. "Dashed good. We shall probably all get gongs in the New Year Honours List. I shall pass over the head of Marriot into a fine post as Counsellor. What will you choose, Methuen?"

"My pension and a small flat in London," said Methuen who was apt to take things literally. "But," he added lamely, "I could have had either these ten years."

"Ah!" said Porson pointing a scraggy finger. "You are a work mystic. You cannot stop working. Must go on. You will end with ulcers and a knighthood."

"I don't know," said Methuen with a twinkle. "I wouldn't mind that either." All of a sudden he felt an immense weariness as he thought of the hills outside there, in the heart of Serbia, with their secret; he heard the echo of the rivers as they bored their way through the gorges, throwing up spray. How beautiful a place it was! Yet sudden death might lurk at every corner. "Me for bed," he said, though he was unwilling to leave the comfortable arm-chair.

That night Carter was surprised and somewhat touched to find him kneeling by his bed in prayer, dressed in his coarse, faded woollen pyjamas with the brown stripe. "I just came in to see that you were all right," he said apologetically. "Yes," said Methuen, "I was just saying my prayers. Always have done it since I was a child. I never sleep well if I don't."

## Further Perplexities

"Prayers!" said Carter to himself, getting into bed and switching off the light. "Well, he'll need some prayers where he's going."

# CHAPTER SEVEN

# The Picture Gallery

The morning dawned fine, and Mr. Judson permitted himself the luxury of an early morning bathe in the river before breakfast, driving out in Carter's car to a point beyond the town. Carter himself lay in bed making incoherent noises and refused to share in this exploit, and it must be admitted that he showed little shame when Judson reappeared at the breakfast-table to crack his egg with an air of triumphant virtue. "I'm not as badly out of condition as I thought," he told his host. "I swam about a mile in a very tough current." Carter shook his head: "After forty, my dear chap," he said, "one must play safe. Or one springs a sprocket. Early rising is for the young."

"When were you forty?" asked Mr. Judson.

"Two years from now," said Carter.

They drove to the Embassy in great good humour and once more Mr. Judson locked himself in with the account books—which he handled for all the world as if they were rare, and slightly disgusting palimpsests. Somehow the thought of meeting Vida had displaced his preoccupation with the Serbian folk-songs; she might offer him the clue to them and save him further cogitation. He whistled softly to himself as he copied out those which had been repeated. Even the Ambassador, it

seemed, was in a good humour. There was a little note on his
desk which he opened with some surprise, marvelling at the
fine lacework of the handwriting on the envelope: "My dear
Colonel," he read, "nothing would have pleased me better than
to have you to a meal despite the view I take of your mission
here. Nevertheless since you are masquerading as a clerk I feel
it would be bad policy to draw you into the limelight by inviting you to my table. I trust you will not mistake discretion for
churlishness."

"Very decent of him," said Methuen, "considering."

He showed the letter to Porson who chuckled and said:
"Maybe he has discovered that you fish."

"By the way: this rendezvous——"

"Yes?"

"Can I borrow your raincoat and beret?"

Porson put on a long-suffering air and said: "Take them,
dear old spy-catcher. They are in the hall."

"And will you drop me off in some odd corner of the town
so that I am not followed?"

"On one condition."

"What?"

"That if she is beautiful you introduce me."

"Ah," said Methuen. "She is: I wish I could."

"I've always wanted a beautiful spy."

The fat and snouty figure of Marriot appeared in the Chancery doorway. "Ah," he said with ineffable condescension. "Ah,
Methuen, everything all right I hope?"

"Yes," said Methuen gravely.

"I'm glad. Of course you must feel a bit out of it with
H.E.'s uncompromising attitude to your work, but you know
how it is in diplomacy." He smiled as amiably as he could
and rubbed his hands. "We have to be extra careful, extra
careful."

# The Picture Gallery

The change in his attitude was rather marked and Methuen turned to Porson when the door closed and said: "There seems to be a slightly different attitude to-day. The natives are less hostile."

"They are getting used to you. Just wait until you muck things up and are brought back on a slab."

"God forbid," said Methuen not without a touch of superstition.

"Come along," said Porson. "Time to be moving."

They climbed into his battered old racing-car which he drove with great skill and raced away across the town. Despite the fact that they did not seem to be followed, Porson took no chances and for twenty minutes they doubled about the town, crossing and re-crossing their tracks until in a wilderness of alleys in the area above the Sava Bridge Methuen asked to be put down. He had by this time put on Porson's mackintosh and beret.

He turned down a street and crossed to the Knez Mihaelova, pausing from time to time to gaze into a shop window. The park, by comparison with the mean streets and bare shop windows, looked singularly inviting and he crossed the asphalt paths towards the little picture-gallery with a light and springy step. Here and there, to be sure, he spotted a blue-clad militia man and not infrequently a "leather man" (as Porson called the secret policemen), but he was sure that their attention was not focused on him, and he only hoped that Vida had managed to arrive at the rendezvous without difficulty. He bought a ticket to the exhibition which commemorated the Partisan War and entered the gallery with the crowd. His heart gave a little leap for he saw her directly, standing in the far corner of the gallery examining a painting. He opened his catalogue and worked his way slowly towards her, gravely examining each picture in turn with a judicial eye. It was not long before they found themselves standing together before a particularly flamboyant representation of the fourth offensive and Vida whispered: "Go up to the tower of the fort. I will follow."

With the same unhurried air of concentration he did as he was told, working his way out of the gallery and turning to the left, across the expanse of gravel to the steps which led up into the old tower. The path led them across a sort of ravelin and through a gate towards the central bastion, and here he climbed the stairs slowly, pausing from time to time to take in the magnificent view which changed from room to room. A few couples sauntered in the sun on the terrace, and some children played about in one of the courtyards, but for the most part the fort seemed more or less deserted. He tucked himself in a corner of the battlements and stared out at the confluence of the two rivers which swirled away round the foot of the Kalemigdan. The Danube and the Sava met in a single jointless ripple beyond the Sava Bridge and swept down, turbid and brown, towards the eastern flank of the city.

Here Vida joined him in a little while and putting her arm round his shoulders stood beside him as he gazed out over the soft purple plain which stretched away towards Hungary. "Is it not lovely?" she said. Anyone who saw them might imagine they were husband and wife, pausing for a rest and for the first time he saw a smile of unshadowed content on her face. The old Vida was coming alive.

"Why are you working for them?" said Methuen at last when the first of her few questions had been asked and answered. "Ah," she said, "the only choice left was to become the mistress of someone. My ration card was taken away because I refused. One has to eat. But luckily, luckily . . . I found I could be of use." She lowered her voice to a whisper again and said: "They are afraid of us, Methuen. They know we are getting strong. They know that everyone is on our side and that the country would rise to-morrow if it could hear the voice of a leader."

"Tell me about the broadcasts," said Methuen, drawing a bow at a venture, and was delighted to see the look of surprised recognition in her eyes. "Ah! you know about those," she said.

"A certain amount. Sophia Maric must be a White Eagle too."

"How do you find out things that even the OZNA does not know?"

"How is the message passed?"

"Some are repeated."

"I know."

"The message starts at the tenth line."

Methuen could have kicked himself with annoyance. He should really have thought of something as simple as that. With a sudden impulse he took out of his pocket the little collection of folk-songs which Anson had carried with him on his journey. He hunted out the passage marked in pencil and was delighted to find that it started at the tenth line of the poem.

"What is that?" said Vida. "Is something wrong?"

"I'm an ass," said Methuen "I should have known."

"I should not tell you this," she said, squeezing his arm through the sleeve of his mackintosh. "I am sworn to secrecy. The eagles would kill me. I told you that they hate England now, nearly as much as they hate Tito. They do not understand you like I do. Methuen, help us."

"How?" he said helplessly. "Just how?"

She turned her dark magnificent eyes on him and said: "At this very moment our movement needs help. We need access to the highest quarters in England. Can you reach perhaps the Prime Minister with a message if you wish?"

"I doubt it."

"It is important for England too. Something very big is happening in the mountains of south Serbia. We have the means in our hands to overturn the Tito régime. Surely England would be interested in that? I remember when I worked for you you could always reach the Secretary of State's office. Our people are savage, they don't trust England. They think that if you knew what we had discovered you would help Tito to suppress our movement. Oh, Methuen, do you see?"

"What is it?" Tears came into her eyes and she shook her head. "I cannot tell you without authority. I must not. I dare not."

There came the tramp of feet on the turret stairs and she broke off. A large family party, surrounded by children, rambled up to the terrace with much puffing and blowing, and admired the view with considerable expenditure of oaths and grunts. Gravely the father pointed out the sights to his children: "There is Smederavo—or should be if you could see it," and "There is Zemun—only it is hidden in smoke. . . ." Methuen could feel the girl trembling, and glancing at her out of the corner of his eye he saw that she was crying noiselessly. She recovered herself and blew her nose. The Serbian family rambled off and silence fell once more.

"I'm going to-morrow," he said.

"To London?"

"Yes."

"How I wish I could come with you. But I feel I must see this thing through to the end. In spite of being brought up abroad I feel so terribly Serbian here," and she pressed her hand to her heart with an old familiar gesture that gave Methuen a pang of sympathy. "You too loved our country, before, Methuen. Have you seen what they are doing to it?"

Silence fell for a moment during which they stood gazing out across the magnificent sweep of the two rivers. Then she said: "Methuen, I have decided one thing. To-night we have a secret meeting and I shall ask permission to tell you what we are doing. Just one phrase will make it clear to you. Believe me, it is nothing small. But I only do this if you promise to go to the Foreign Secretary yourself and tell him that England must help us. Will you? Will you?"

"I promise you with all my heart," said Methuen, using the lovely Serbian phrase with an emotion that surprised him, "that I will try. I promise you." She took his hand and kissed it. "To-night," she said, "after twelve, you may telephone the number I am giving you. Ask for Sophia Maric. Ask her if Vida is there and if I have the permission of my people I will say one phrase to you which will contain the whole meaning. You will understand then."

She produced a diminutive powder-puff and restored her complexion, saying as she did so: "I must go now. I cannot tell you what a pleasure it was to see you; like a visit to honest old England, Methuen. I know you will not fail us. But I must ask permission from my people."

She turned and was gone from sight before Methuen could struggle out of the grip of his emotions and face the inadequacy of language to express how deeply moved he was. Walking back across the green lawns, and through the shabby streets of the town to the Embassy he repeated to himself again and again: "What the devil can it be?"

Nor was the goggle-eyed Porson much help when he heard the story. "I bet you it's uranium," he said after many perplexed guesses. "But what use would that be?"

"Uranium?" said Methuen with resignation. "What use would that be to Vida and her crowd?"

Porson made a vague sweeping gesture with his arm. "Oh, I don't know," he said, "everybody seems to want the stuff."

"Young man," said Methuen severely, "don't waste my

time with nonsense guesses. Leave me to work on the messages
a bit. If we are starting to-morrow we haven't much time. And
besides Vida may put the secret into our hands to-night."

He retired once more to Mr. Judson's little den and impatiently sweeping aside the account books took out some
paper and pencils from the drawer. He had already marked the
repeat-poems which, according to Vida, carried the message,
and it was the work of a moment to arrange them in chrono-
logical order and underline each tenth line. Apart from the
fragment already quoted, he assembled the following quota-
tions:

> *O King beset by shapes innumerable*
> *As the dead, you must not leave*
> *Unless your birthright goes with you,*
> *And that is ours.*

> *The King's secret touchstone*
> *We have discovered, but many*
> *Are the whispers and grave*
> *The dangers, speed alone will help him.*

> *Help for the King will come*
> *By four-footed friends,*
> *Caravans to carry his tokens,*
> *And turn his shame to victory.*

> *In the month of the magpie*
> *He must set forth in a hedge of muskets*
> *Seeking the sea where*
> *Help will await him.*

These fragments he typed out in several copies, giving one
to Porson and one to Carter so that each might work indepen-

dently on them. Porson became tremendously solemn and stared at them through his eyeglass. "My dear fellow," he said hopelessly, "I was never any good at riddles. But this mass of highly metaphorical Slav guff simply defeats me." Methuen said: "Try. Think about it a little. Let us all have dinner tonight and see if we can make anything of it."

His own elation had given place to gloom, for it had suddenly struck him that they might be trying to break a prearranged code—that the meaning might not lie in the actual verses themselves. Each verse might stand for a message already agreed upon; in which case no amount of thought could unriddle these oracular utterances. Nevertheless something was plain—the talk of a king's "birthright", "touchstone", etc., did seem to have some relation to Vida's statement about something the White Eagles had discovered; something perhaps they had been hunting for.

At dinner that evening neither he nor his colleagues had successfully interpreted the riddle. Porson suggested that "four-footed friends" might mean horses, but this was his only contribution to the discussion. Carter plainly declared his mind to be a blank and added disarmingly: "But then it always has been whenever you pushed some poetry under my nose. Ever since I was a nipper."

There was nothing to do except to wait upon the telephone-call which might offer them the key to the mystery. "I'm sorry to have turned into a club-bore," said Methuen, "but these problems are tremendously exciting and they grip you. I must confess, though, that apart from the 'month of the magpie' which is June, I can't make any progress."

It seemed wiser to shelve the whole business for a time as Carter was showing some disposition to yawn and fidget. After dinner they played a round or two of rummy and listened to the news. Carter owned an excellent collection of classical records, and played them some until it was time to telephone. This they planned to do from an outside call-box, as the chances of the wire being tapped were less. Porson knew of one by the tram stop at the end of the road, and accordingly the three of them set out to walk the distance at a leisurely pace. As they crossed the garden and passed through the front gate Methuen saw a figure stir in the darkness on the opposite side of the road. "Ah yes," said Carter following his glance, "we all have leather men attached to us. One gets used to them." They walked down the rough badly cobbled street between the trees; only one in three street lamps were alight and whole stretches of the street were in total darkness. "It wouldn't be difficult to shake him off," said Methuen, but Carter shrugged his shoulders. "Why bother?" he said. "I always take a stroll after dinner and he's used to the idea."

They skirted the dark line of villas and descended the hill. The tram stop was well lit, though at this time of night there were few passengers about. A long line of horse-drawn carts clattered along on the main road which lay between them and the river. Somewhere in the fastnesses of the goods yards an engine shrieked twice and was silent. A light wind sprang up sending little eddies of dust swirling along the cobbled reaches of the road, and ruffling the dense foliage of the trees. They walked from shadow to shadow, and from shadow to shadow the man in the leather coat followed them. "There it is," said Porson, and after covertly glancing at his watch Methuen left them and walked smartly towards the telephone booth. The light was broken and it smelt foully of sunflower-oil. He had to grope with his finger and count the numbers carefully. Excitement gripped him as he heard in the dimness the slight noise of a connection slipping into place and the slow blurred scraping which indicated that somewhere a bell was ringing.

The seconds lengthened themselves eternally in the stillness.

Perhaps he had the wrong number? Perhaps he had memorized it wrongly. A thousand and one possibilities sprang into his mind, yet he quietly ignored them and held on to the chipped receiver waiting for the ringing to stop and for a voice to answer. His stillness communicated itself to the other two who stood outside the box, quietly smoking. The man in the leather coat retired discreetly to a pool of shadow and was swallowed up in it.

There was a faint click and then a voice spoke: "Hullo." Methuen spoke hoarsely. "Please, Madam, may I speak to Miss Sophia Maric?" There was a moment of hesitation as if the person at the other end was gathering her forces together. Then she said: "This is Comrade Maric speaking."

"Then be so kind as to let me speak to Vida if she is there."

The answer came like a blow in the face.

"Vida is dead."

There was the faint dry click of the receiver as it was put down—like the snapping of a stalk of celery—and Methuen was left holding the black receiver in his trembling fingers. A thousand suppositions flooded into his mind as he stood there. Then in a fury he dialled the number again and again stood listening to the faint purring note of a distant bell ringing. "Vida is dead." The words kept echoing in his mind with monotonous iteration. "She can't be," he said to himself, furiously. The bell rang on and on.

Then at last there came a click and a man's voice answered, as if drugged with sleep. "Hullo," Methuen said, "I want to speak to Sophia Maric please. It is urgent."

The answering voice sank into a deeper register as it said: "There is no one of that name here. You have the wrong number."

Methuen walked slowly out into the street, feeling dazed and numb. He joined his two companions in their stroll back to the house, and to their eager whispered questions he could only repeat helplessly: "They say Vida is dead."

They returned to the house in silence and sank into the cretonne-covered arm-chairs of the drawing-room in attitudes of despondency. Carter mixed them a whisky and soda with a solicitude which showed that he knew how deep a shock Methuen had sustained. "And yet it's not possible," Porson burst out. "Who would kill her? Why?"

Methuen sighed: "You see the nature of the thing we are up against. Obviously there is something big brewing and the suggestion that she should let the British Government in on it has alarmed the White Eagles. So they've. . . ." He had difficulty in getting the word out: "Murdered her. Or locked her up. God knows."

"Alternatively," said Carter, "the OZNA might have tumbled to her. They are morbidly suspicious of their own employees. Everyone is double checked. She may have given herself away."

"Yes," said Methuen. "Yes." A savage fury was rising in him. "Poor Vida."

It was lucky that there was still much to do to prepare for to-morrow's journey. It would take his mind off the subject.

He got up and went to his room where he wrapped his clothes and equipment in a parcel and gave them to Porson who would be driving the car. Then he sat down and composed a long despatch for Dombey, setting out the new material with which he had been faced and asking him to have the problem followed up from the London end as quickly as possible. Carter was still in the living-room reading when he returned. "Can I count on you," he said, "to send this signal to Dombey about to-night's little affair? It is quite up to date, I told him about the 'phone call." Carter nodded.

"And Carter——"

"Yes."

"If you lose track of me for goodness' sake promise not to raise any hue and cry with the Government until a full ten days has gone by without a message from me. If I am on to something good it may take time, and a sudden hunt for me by the OZNA might spoil everything."

Carter hesitated. "Very well," he said at last, "though it won't be easy to restrain H.E. He flaps terribly."

"You must try. I'm determined to get to the bottom of this business if I have to take out residence papers and stay for the rest of my life."

"All right old man," said Carter gently. He was thinking of Anson: of the body he had helped to carry feet first through the Chancery door: a huddled figure covered in an old army ground-sheet. His friend had spent one night upon the map-laden table of the office before the local mortuary would take him in. And then all the trouble and fuss to find a carpenter to make a coffin.

"Go to bed and get some sleep," he said, standing up and putting his arm on the elder man's shoulder. "You have a hell of a day ahead of you."

He locked Methuen's draft in the little wall-safe and turned out the light. From the window-sill he retrieved the bowl of flowers in which the thoughtful OZNA had placed a microphone little larger than a bee. It was gagged. "Shall we pass them a message before we turn in?" he said, but Methuen was in no mood for humour. "I should disconnect it," he said. "Ah, but then they'll stick another one somewhere. At least I know where this one is," said Carter, fondling the bowl lovingly.

Methuen grunted and said good night. As he undressed he said to himself under his breath: "Vida is dead." Yet somehow he could not believe it; yet who could doubt that it was true?

He slept.

## CHAPTER EIGHT

# *Journey Into the Hills*

I t was still dark when the little green alarm-clock beside the bed set up its discreet purring and woke Methuen from a sleep which had been relatively calm and dreamless. Sitting up in bed at the brink of day he felt like a diver poised above a pool. Soon he must dive into the unknown waters of adventure. Where they would carry him he did not know; but action was a relief from too much meditation. It brought into play a different side of his character, the part where experience and will took over from doubt and conjecture; where the buccaneer took over from the comparatively timid and law-abiding person he was.

Carter came into his room with a cup of tea and found him shaving with methodical care, whistling softly under his breath as he did so. The young major noticed a new spareness, a new litheness in his movements as he walked to the window and drew the curtains on the darkness which would soon be lifting.

"What time is it light?"

In June the light comes relatively early and as they walked across the dew-drenched grass of the garden the first streaks of yellow began to touch the eastern sky. Carter started up the engine of his car with a harsh clatter that woke the sentry in the makeshift sentry-box at the end of the road. He let in the clutch and they went swaying carefully down the pot-holed road towards the Sava, crossed the tram-lines and turning right, gathered speed along the tree-lined avenue which led them to the Embassy. The morning air was deliciously damp and fresh with the moisture of the river flowing out of sight among the trees to their left, scoring out its path in the rich alluvial mud of the Serbian plain.

There were no cars on the road, but they encountered a long procession of sleepy drays bringing their wretched freight into the markets of the capital: for the most part consignments of maize cobs for bread. Their drivers sat like comatose owls on the seats wrapped in their torn clothes against the early morning chill; while in many carts lay a sprawl of women and children, frowsily sleeping. Carter drove expertly but in silence, for which Methuen was grateful as it gave him time to collect and marshal his inner resources for the adventure which lay ahead.

In the foreground of his thoughts too rose the figure of Vida —the dark beseeching eyes which silently implored his belief in a cause which everyone deemed dead—freedom. Thinking of those candid and ingenuous eyes, and of that rich friendly personality Methuen almost forgot how wretched the cause she advocated was; it was certainly better than what existed at present here—but would it prove any less of a disappointment if once it should triumph? He could not tell. He could only say that the present was unjust, cruel and dedicated to death.

Porson and Carter arrived simultaneously at the Embassy and raced round the drive together before leaving their cars in the car park. Then the three of them made their way to the side entrance and pressed the brass bell-push. A sleepy night-guard peered at them through a brass socket for a second and let them in; he was in his shirt and trousers, and had been sleeping in an arm-chair in the hall.

"Now then," said Porson, "to business. Hubbard, will you make us a cup of coffee and bring it to my office?"

"Yessir."

Porson adjusted his monocle and sat down in a leather arm-chair, throwing one lanky leg over the other, and placing the tips of his fingers together. "Mark me well," he said with the air of a celebrated K.C. summing up for a suburban jury, "the duty car we use is in the garage at the back of the Embassy. There is a back entrance which I'll show you. You'll lie down in the back and cover up. Presently I'll appear at the front entrance, whistling nonchalantly, and drive the car round to the Chancery entrance to pick up Blair, the clerk who is coming with us. Then we are away. At the last check-point beyond Avala we shall slow down and flourish our travel-permit, there will be a rapid counting of heads (keep yours down) and then we'll be waved through. A hundred yards after that a large black Buick, packed to the gunwales with gibbering analphabetic policemen, will slide out from behind a bush and follow us. You can then emerge and do your toilet at leisure, trans-form yourself into whatever sort of creature you wish, before propelling yourself into the bog as per schedule."

"Where is my gear?"

"Already in the car."

"My trout-rod?"

"Yes. Yes," said Porson testily and raising his eyes to heaven moved his lips in soundless prayer for a moment; then, appar-ently addressing his Creator, he said: "I ask you. All he bothers about is his trout-rod. What has SOq done to deserve such single-minded egoists?"

There was still a little time to spare while Blair and the clerks made up the bag for the Skoplje Consulate. They drank their coffee to the accompaniment of a running battery of waggish remarks by Porson who seemed a trifle light-headed—perhaps it was due to the early hour at which he had been forced to rise.

"Well," he said at last.

"I'm ready," said Methuen, and there was music in his step as he followed the lanky secretary down the corridor into the Residence, and down the stone stairs to the cellar; here they branched left and traversed the large handsome billiard-room and ballroom combined until they reached the kitchen. From a corner a small green door opened directly into the dark garage. "Here," said Porson. The huge Mercedes lay like a noble old ship at anchor in the darkness. Methuen cast a quick appraising eye over her. Old she certainly was, but her power-ful engine and heavy springing made her a most suitable trans-port for the sort of roads one encountered in Serbia and Mace-donia.

He shed his coat and waistcoat and shoes and handing them to Porson he climbed into the back and lay down on the floor. A rug was spread over him and Porson said: "Now not a word." The green door closed with a bang and Methuen lay in the darkness smelling the odour of polish and petrol which had impregnated the air. He had not long to wait, however, for presently he heard steps approach on the asphalt drive and the main doors of the garage rumbled back on their grooves. Whistling (though just how nonchalantly he could not see), Porson climbed aboard and started up the engine. Its deep satisfying murmur blotted out everything. The car rolled smoothly out into the drive and drew up at the Chancery office entrance where Blair was waiting with the white sack over his arm.

"All aboard!" cried Porson, and they were soon booming along the streets of the capital, slithering in tram-lines and bouncing among the pot-holes of the main road. Porson drove with an erratic swiftness, and to the accompaniment of much cursing and swearing as he grazed the backs of buses or drove pedestrians in flocks out of the path by the power of the old-fashioned klaxon with which the car was equipped.

"Don't hit anything, Mr. Porson," said Blair nervously. "We should have had it then." He was a pale freckled north country-man. Porson tossed back his head and said: "Psaw! Me hit any-thing? I've got a clean licence, Blair. Fear nothing."

They were racing along the winding roads which lead south through the pleasant rolling pastures and woodlands where the dark bulk of Avala Hill rears itself from the flat plain. The old Mercedes got into her stride and the powerful six-cylinder engine settled down to a smooth continuous purring note which bespoke power. Dawn was coming up fast now and Methuen wished he could watch the remembered landscape of his student days unroll once more on either side of him. It was hot under the rug. They swept through a number of small sleepy villages and up to the foot of the fir-crowned hill before Porson said, over his shoulder: "Now for the counting of heads, Methuen, and we are through."

A blue-clad militiaman appeared in the road holding a white wooden signal in his hand. Porson slowed down to give him time to see the diplomatic number-plates of the car, while Blair leaned from the window holding out his documents. The policeman nodded and stepped back. They were through. The Mercedes gathered power again and they raced round the crown of the hill where the road drops steeply to the plain. "Now for the escort," said Porson, and as they flashed past a side-turning a long sleek Buick edged itself into the road and started out in pursuit of them. "Why there should always be four people in it," said Blair, "I can't see." Porson grunted. "They can't come for the ride," he said and once more turning his head back added: "Methuen, you can get up now. We are all set."

## Journey into the Hills

Methuen rose stiffly from the floor and sank on to the cushions of the back seat with a sigh. The back of the car was closed and the side-screens were up, making it impossible for the following car to see into the interior of the Mercedes. They still had several hours to go before they reached the Ibar valley, and he set himself methodically to sort his kit and to dress. They had started much earlier than usual so that he should have as much daylight as possible ahead of him when once the jump into the unknown had been made.

As he pulled on the heavy riding-boots he gazed out at the early morning landscape, the green rolling country that swept away southward towards the dark mountains which as yet were simply mauve smudges upon the skyline. They were able to make good time along the excellent metalled highway which leads out in a series of graceful curves and loops towards Topola, rising like a swallow through cuttings and dipping in and out among the richly-cultivated hills. Vineyards stretched away on either side of them and Methuen could not resist giving Porson a short lecture on the Serbian wines he had once studied with affectionate care. This was a celebrated part of the wine country. "Out of bounds alas!" said Porson, "or I should by now have collected enough material for a monograph. We get inferior stuff in town!"

The black Buick held on to them, staying always about three hundred yards behind. Methuen took a peep at it through the curtained window. "They are awfully close," he said, and Porson smiled a knowing smile as he answered: "Wait till the dust begins. They have to eat our dust all the way into Macedonia. You should see them when we arrive at Skoplje—as if they were all wearing powdered wigs and false moustaches. Don't worry, Methuen. We'll have plenty of time."

Methuen smoked and pondered as the great car whistled onwards. His fishing-rod and the bulkier part of his equipment he had wrapped in the light bed-roll. Into the various pockets and slings of his magnificent coat he had placed his pistol and compass, some solid fuel, a half-pint Thermos, and his beloved *Walden*. "By God," said Porson, "anyone would think you were going to stay for months." "I am," said Methuen grimly. The sun was quite hot by now and Porson said approvingly: "There's going to be a hell of a lot of dust. Good show!"

They swayed and scrambled through the cobbled streets of Mladenovac and whistled out into the countryside beyond. The Buick came smoothly on behind. Blair produced some biscuits and an excellent bottle of white wine which they shared. Their spirits rose, but behind the fooling of Porson Methuen sensed a tension and a reserve which had been absent before. For his part, though he looked out at that smiling landscape with familiar pleasure recaptured in memory, he felt the dark wings of danger spreading themselves above them—and out of it all the thought of Vida's death rose up to afflict him, leaving him with a slow-burning resentment and determination.

"You won't forget to ring up Belgrade," he said, "and drop any messages there are for me in the ditch as per arrangement." Porson nodded. "On my way back. We'll start at midnight and be with you just before light."

Half-way between Mladenovac and Kralevo the road began to deteriorate into patches of pitted cobbles, and then as they swept round a wooded curve Porson said: "Now watch this." The asphalt abruptly ceased and the car wallowed on to the pitted country road of dust and loose stones. A cloud arose round them which powdered the lower branches of the trees. "Look behind," said Porson gleefully. Methuen did so. They were throwing up a smoke-screen of bilious yellow dust— impenetrable in volume. "God," he said, with genuine pity for the Buick-load of police which followed them. "From here on

they drop about a quarter of a mile behind," said Porson gleefully. "Sometimes we annoy them by slowing up too."

Kralevo passed in a cloud and the note of the car changed as
they headed across the plain for the mountain-range which now
loomed up at them from the south; the river sprawled to the
left of them gleaming green and yellow in the flat plain. The
road and river converged slowly upon the looming shadowy
gorge which marked the entrance to the Ibar valley. "Pretty
soon now," said Porson in a voice which betrayed an ill-
controlled excitement. Methuen puffed quietly at his cigarette
before tossing it out of the window.

At the entrance of the sullen gorge, where the mountains
rise to right and left, the road, railway and river, having con-
ducted a seemingly endless flirtation, are suddenly squeezed
together and pass through the narrow rock entrance side by
side. Here the Ibar becomes swift, brown and turbid; giant
poplars and willows, their roots gripping the shaly banks like
knuckles, shade the whole length of the road. The air becomes
dense with the smell of water, for several smaller rivers have
cut their way through the mountain to empty themselves into
the Ibar, and the crumbling rocky walls which flank the gorge
are bursting with freshwater springs. The valley for all its
gloom is alive with the ripple of bird-song which mingles with
the thunder of the Ibar's waters as they roar down towards
Rashka.

The railway looked like a toy. It had been cut in the side of
the mountain and the tracks passed through a series of rock-
tunnels each of which was closely guarded by pickets. Methuen
saw the diminished figures of these guards walking along the
stone parapet, stopping to gaze down curiously at the car as it
passed. Each section of tunnel had its own patrol, and the
soldiers lounged in the sun on the stone balconies, idly smoking
or tossing pebbles into the swift waters of the Ibar below.

"What about them?" said Methuen, and Porson said quickly: "The part where you jump is completely enclosed with greenery. They can't see. Only when you climb the hill you'll have to keep out of sight. Look, a train!"

They heard a series of muffled shrieks and a heavy rumbling across the river. The guards came to life and took up position. The rumbling increased in volume and finally an absurdly toy-like train emerged from the rock-tunnel with a puff of grey smoke—as if it had been fired from the mouth of a gun. It rolled slowly across the balcony-like parapet, trailing a long banner of sooty dust and smoke, and with a catarrhal whistle plunged once more into the rock, its wheels making a hard resonant noise, as of a billiard ball being rolled across a stone floor. Sixty yards later, before the tail of the train had come into view on the first parapet, the engine emerged once more with another cough. "In and out of the rock," said Porson, "like a needle in cloth."

"Hard work cutting that railway," said Methuen with mild professional interest; the river looked too strong for any swimmer. "It's well guarded," said Porson, "though one good burst in a tunnel. . . ."

They rolled onwards between the flickering crowns of the trees which reached up at the road from the river bank. Behind them the yellow cloud of dust volleyed away down the road reducing visibility to nothing. Yellowhammers and magpies frolicked in the trees, and here and there the stern rock-faces to their right stood back and fanned away into dome-like mountains, steeply clad with beech and fir, and showing small pockets of cultivation. A crumbling Frankish fortress dominated one height and Methuen caught the flicker of sunlight on something which might have been the barrel of a gun at the eastern corner. He had a small but powerful pair of glasses in his kit but there was no time to train them on this tempting target. "There's a company of soldiers up in the fort," said Porson. "They supply the pickets for the railway. Two machine-guns. Nothing heavier."

He was gradually reducing speed and the great car rolled effortlessly along the beautiful river road, in and out of the shadows thrown by the trees. They turned a corner and the fort was swallowed; and here the trees grew in great clusters, chestnut and eucalyptus raising their dusty crowns to the sky. "We're coming to it," said Porson; round the next corner there was a white milestone by a ruined signalman's hut which was their marker. "All set," said Methuen quietly and gripped his bed-roll as he let down the massive window of the car. "Do you see it?" The milestone climbed out of the mauve shadows of the rock-face and came towards them like a pointing finger. "Let her go. Good luck!" cried Porson. Methuen gave a heave and tossed his bed-roll into the ditch; then opening the door he plunged out after it into the deep grass, slipping and sliding to the bottom as the great car gathered speed and covered him in a cloud of pungent dust. Porson gave a hoot on the klaxon which echoed like the wild cry of some solitary bird among the rocks.

# CHAPTER NINE

## *The Lone Fisherman*

Methuen lay against the steep bank, his face pressed to the moist grass for what seemed hours. The noise of the Mercedes died away gradually and was replaced by the roaring of the Ibar in its stony bed. The cloud of dust thinned gradually and began to settle, while out of a neighbouring tree came the clear fluting notes of bird-song. He felt his own heart beating against the moist cool grass. Would the police car never come? He strained his ears for the sound of its engines; his heavy duffle coat was warm. A cricket chirped in the grass beside him. Then, after what seemed an age, he heard the whistle of the Buick's engine which gradually increased. "They're taking it pretty easily," he said to himself. The car swept round the corner and he heard its radio playing a Viennese waltz. Then he was engulfed once more in the impenetrable wall of white dust and taking advantage of it he climbed to his feet, gathered up his bed-roll and galloped for the cover of the trees.

Within a hundred yards of where he had jumped a narrow gorge opened at right-angles to the main river-gorge and here the swift and shallow Studenitsa river rolled and tumbled from a series of rock-balconies, covered with slippery moss, to join the larger river. The air was dense with spray, and the trees leaned out of the sheer cliff at all angles. The cover here was plentiful and good, and avoiding the mule-track Methuen climbed deliberately up beside the river, slipping and sliding on the loose surface of leaf-mould, and pushing his way through the dense clusters of tree-ferns towards the summit, eight hundred feet above.

The going was hard but in the clear spray-drenched air of the valley he felt his spirits rise. From time to time he paused for a breather, gazing from some small clearing of greenery to where the road below him ran like a white scar beside the black river. At one point he came out on a spur overlooking the mule-track and saw a group of peasants driving two ox-carts loaded with wood down towards the valley. As far as his memory served him, there were only two small hamlets along the Stud-enitsa river, and the only human activity apart from land cultivation centred about a sawmill which flanked the monastery at the summit. Here he had camped once beside the smooth river and fished away the better part of a summer with a Serbian friend. In the evening they had walked up to the sawmill to drink plum-brandy with the monks and peasants and to share the fishing gossip of the community. Here too they had experimented with different ways of cooking trout, and he remembered clearly the taste of fish baked in the sour cream called *kaimak* which serves the peasant for butter.

But these memories did not cause him to relax his vigilance and he moved along in the shadow of the fir trees, keeping the river in sight but never venturing out into the open. In half an hour he had reached the summit and here the river broadened with the valley, while the hills opened into deeply indented upland valleys traversed by delicious footpaths which circled the squares of luxuriant maize and the dappled hayfields which lay open to the afternoon sunlight.

Here the oak forests ran down to the water's edge and he

could walk on grass richly studded with flowers. The world seemed empty of human beings. To the east a flock of sheep grazed without a shepherd who was doubtless fishing in the shadowy river below the sawmill. Here too he came upon orchards full of plum trees and hedges riotous with blackberries so large that in spite of himself he stopped to gather some. Away to the left, hidden by a shoulder of hill, lay the monastery, and from this direction he could hear the whimper of a saw; but he gave it a wide berth and struck up the valley, guided by his memories of a summer he had believed forgotten. He himself was rather astonished by the accuracy of his memory, for in his enchanted valley nothing seemed to have changed. In the silence the river ran on with its gentle rattle of water stirring pebbles—a pearly shadow of sound against which the songs of the birds rose bright and poignant on the moist air. The hedges were thick with a variety of flowers, and his quick eye detected the presence of old friends, yellow snapdragon, sky-blue flax. Here the hills ran away in a series of verdant undulations to where, softly painted against the sky, the towering mountains of central Serbia rose, lilac and green and red; and in all this lovely country there were no signs of life, no mule-teams raising dust, no bands of armed men watching from the woods. It baffled him to imagine how Anson could have got himself into trouble here, the going was so easy, the points of visibility so many, the cover so good.

The sun was still high enough to be hot and he was still sweating profusely from the steep climb, so he bathed his face in the icy river, and allowed himself a five-minute rest in a copse while he examined the hills around him with his glasses. There was little enough to interest him. Against one remote skyline he caught sight of oxen ploughing, and to the east he picked up a peasant house with pointed gables, but for the rest the world looked newly born: unpopulated. Yet here and there were large areas of maize and barley growing which argued the presence of husbandmen, and the sheep tinkled their way across the pastures to the north of him. High up in the cloudless June sky an eagle hovered. The light skirmishing wind blew puff-balls and bits of straw across the river.

Around one wooded curve of the river he came upon a solitary monk fishing under a tree and was forced to climb the hill from the back in order not to pass him, but even he hardly communicated a sense of life to the landscape in which he sat so motionless, back against a tree, his rod propped between his knees. Perhaps he was sleeping. Methuen watched him for a while from a clump of maize-stalks hoping to see him hook a fish, but in vain. The river ran as smoothly under his line as the grass upon which he sat. From time to time a nut dropped off the tree into the water. "Dry fishing," said Methuen to himself, "that's the real ticket," and scanned the dimpled waters to see what the fish were rising to: but this was the wildest self-indulgence and he pulled himself together.

His objective was a series of fairly large caves in the opposite bank of the river where it entered a ravine of red and yellow conglomerate. Here he had sheltered once from the rain, and here he hoped to find a ready-made headquarters where he might dump his equipment before embarking on a methodical exploration of the range of hills. Accordingly he left the trees and waded across the water at a ford, and struck a narrow overgrown path which led him gradually upwards into the thick scrub which choked the entrance to the gorge.

There were, as far as he could see, no other fishermen about and this was surprising for it was at this point that the Studen-itsa river became really fishable. Two great prongs of stone bounded the water, and here for a good way the river itself seemed all but choked by a solid floor of branches which had been washed down from the mountains above, and which had been covered by a dense carpet of green moss. Here too were huge boulders against which the water raised itself in dark pools, thrown up to right and left of its course. Peering down into the inky recesses of these pools Methuen discerned the large shadows of fishes, lounging among the shadows. But he must not indulge himself in this way, he kept telling himself, as he followed the path along the precipitous sides of the ravine; at one point, from a turn in the track, a corner of the orchard where the monk had been fishing came into view. Methuen glanced back and saw the figure still sitting there, motionless.

He turned and was about to address himself to the path when something about the immobility of the distant figure struck him, some preternatural stillness in the pose which had not altered by a hairbreadth this last hour. Overcome by a sudden impulse he threw his pack behind a bush and turned back on his tracks, running with long strides in his heavy boots down the hill, the scrub snatching at his ankles from either side. He emerged once more behind the hillock, and once more stalked the motionless fisherman.

From the shade of a clump of thick bushes he threw a heavy stone into the stream beside him, disappearing from sight as he did so. The stone crashed into the water startling the fish but the figure of the lone fisherman did not move, and seeing this Methuen cocked his pistol in the shoulder-sling and raced down the slope to the water's edge. He came up beside the figure and knelt down to stare into the dead face with a gradually dawning horror which seemed to communicate itself now to the whole of that silent landscape in which they found themselves, the living man and the dead one.

There was a trickle of blood at his mouth and through the rents of the tattered surplice Methuen could see the cause—the slash of bullet-wounds. He had been shot from directly opposite where the pinewoods came down to the river forming a thick patch of cover. Perhaps he had been asleep, for the body was leaning back against the tree; at all events the sudden death which had come upon him had not disturbed the contemplative serenity of his pose. His rod was propped over a stone and the willow passed beneath his legs as he sat. Round his neck there was a placard on which had been written in clumsy letters: "Traitor". He had, in fact, been nailed to this tree by bullets for all the world like the body of a jay is nailed to a barn door, as a warning. It was presumed that the passer-by would know to whom he had been a traitor, and who had extracted this extreme price for his treachery.

Methuen was like a man awakening suddenly from a dream; the whole of this radiant pristine hill landscape became suddenly filled with shadows and omens. He put out his hand, falteringly, to touch the shoulder of the corpse—as one might put out one's hand to touch a ghost, to see if it were really flesh and blood: and to his horror it slowly toppled over. The conical black hat rolled off into the water and was borne away as swiftly as the fishing-rod of willow. He was an old man, well past sixty. He looked horrible lying there in the sunlight in his tattered soutane.

Methuen, after taking a sounding, crossed the river on a shelf of pebbles and once he was on the opposite bank tried to calculate the firing-position of the assassin. The grass was dense enough for footprints, but higher up the stone side of the bank defeated him. But it was not footprints he was looking for. He cast about like a bloodhound gradually worming his way up the steep bank, holding on to the bushes and hoisting himself up with the branches of trees. Every now and again he took a bearing on the fatal tree which faced him across the river, and after a quarter of an hour he judged himself to be approximately in the firing-position from which the old monk had been shot. He circled among the bushes and at last came upon what he sought—a pile of ejected cartridge-cases—lying at the foot of a fir tree. Turning them over in his fingers he recognized them as the type which is used to feed a sub-machine-gun.

He slipped them into his pocket and after a last glance at the fateful tree with the figure sprawled under it, turned back into the bushes and resumed his journey in the direction of the ravine, full of thoughtfulness. Nor did he turn aside to busy himself with speculations about fishing in those tempting pools, for all of a sudden the woods around seemed to have become peopled by an army of invisible eyes which watched his every movement. This brief attack of nerves he withstood with equanimity; he had often experienced it at the outset of a dangerous operation. But he was grateful in a way for the incident of the dead fisherman as it had awoken him from the feeling of false security into which he had been lulled by the landscape.

He retrieved his pack and followed the twisting path above the river for a few hundred yards until he came to a spur shaded by a huge walnut tree which cast an inky shadow over the cliff; somewhere in this shadow was the entrance to a cave, and he quickened his steps to reach it. The entrance lay at an angle to the main cliff-wall, admirably camouflaged by scrub and the shadow of the tree.

Delighted to find his memory still accurate, he was about to enter the cave-mouth, pistol in hand lest it should already be occupied by a man or an animal, when a thin hissing made him recoil. An enormous yellow viper, flattened among its own dusty coils, barred the entrance. Methuen paused, squinting at it along the sights of his revolver, reluctant to start the tenancy of his new headquarters by firing a shot. The viper hissed once again and its forked tongue flickered in its wicked little head. Methuen stood for a whole minute reflecting. In his heavy boots he had little enough to fear from it and from his memories of the cave he knew that there was a high stone platform which could be used as a bed. If he could live and let live: or rather if the viper could live and let live. . . .

"Now, my beauty," he said coaxingly, "take it easy," and edged his way softly past the reptile into the cave. It hissed again, but did not move, perhaps out of drowsiness, or perhaps because it had eaten a heavy meal of mayflies. Once inside he switched on his torch and confirmed his memories of that long-lost week-end when they had sheltered here from a storm. Here was a wide stone platform, ideally suited for a bed; and here at the farther end was a long fault in the rock which made a natural chimney against which a fire could be lighted. "So far," he said, "so good."

He set to work to put his house in order with the methodical deftness that only long practice can give, ignoring the snake which stayed sunning itself at the mouth of the cave. First he laid out his kit and then, taking a clasp knife, cut himself some branches of greenery for a mattress. The transport of these caused the snake a good deal of alarm, but it was already showing signs of getting used to him and he ignored it, confident that if it did sting him it would never penetrate the heavy boots he wore. His bed made up for the night, he next gathered himself some firewood from a nearby clearing where some trees had been felled, leaving a litter of chips and bark admirable for the purpose. These basic points of housekeeping once settled, he returned to the snake and poured out a few drops of tea from his little Thermos as a peace-offering, but it was obviously a gesture which awoke no comprehension in the reptile for it squirmed away from him, hissing savagely—yet, he thought, more in sorrow than in anger. "All right. All right," he said soothingly and left it to its own devices.

Evening was rapidly settling over the mountains now and having shed all his kit except his pistol and glasses he felt very much more at ease. From the shadow of the cave-mouth he explored the whole terrain with great care, methodically sweeping the mauve contours of the hills. There was no sign of movement, save where the wind ruffled the tree-tops on the crest opposite. He sat quietly on a stone and drank in that quietness, punctuated only by the distant whistle of a train in the stone cuttings above the Ibar river, or the shuffle of maize stalks in the fields below him. The babble of the Studenitsa was silenced by the moss-lined pools into which it curled, and here Methuen saw the fish rising languidly to the flies which dotted the surface.

It was more than human nature could stand, this evidence of the evening rise and hastening back to the cave he unearthed his trout-rod and set off down the slope, solacing his conscience with a lie: "I know it's too dangerous to fish to-night," he said, "but it would be a good idea to assemble my rod and hide it in a convenient place by the river, ready for emergencies." His conscience was not taken in; and indeed when he arrived at the nearest pool he discovered a spot so well hidden from view on every side that he could not resist making what he described to himself as "just a practice cast or two".

In a matter of moments he had a glittering gasping trout beating its life out in the grass upon which he sat, and he was just stuffing it into the pocket of his duffle coat when a rustle in the bushes behind him, but some way up the hill, startled him. He pushed the rod into the bushes and lay for a while behind a bush, nursing his pistol and waiting for developments. But none came, and after a quarter of an hour he eased his cramped knees by crawling swiftly and quietly back to the great tree, feeling the trout wriggling in his pocket all the way.

The snake had retired to bed, and the yellow beam of his torch revealed no sign of it in the cave. He dumped his trout and returned to the entrance with his glasses, deciding to have one final look round before the rapidly approaching darkness made visibility impossible. Bats had begun to flicker against the sky, and from the north came the plaintive whoop of an owl. He sat drinking in the silence and full of that delightful repose which comes only to the camper who knows that he has food, fuel and shelter against the approaching night.

Here and there now came the nocturnal stirrings of animals preparing for the night. A large grey wolf came down to the water to drink and, having lifted its muzzle to sniff the air, looked once or twice in his direction with a distinct anxiety before it turned back out of sight into the dense shrub. A water-rat plopped, and a late-scampering lizard skidded among the rocks.

Methuen suddenly realized that he was tired, and yawning, made his way back to the cave, drawing a screen of branches across the mouth of it. The main chamber where he was to sleep was at right-angles to the entrance so he had no fear that the light of his fire might be observed; while from what he remembered of the rock-chimney, the smoke, which emerged thirty yards higher up the hill where the air-currents were stronger, dispersed at the point of issue.

He had brought a diminutive nest of billies with him which included a small spoked grid upon which he prepared his trout after having let the fire burn up into a heap of soft grey embers; he basted it with some fat scraped from a tin of bully beef and peppered it lightly with some cummin which he had noticed growing near a cottage on his way across the hill. It tasted delicious, and he ate it with his fingers, wiping them on the duffle coat, and having eaten, took a nip at his whisky flask before settling himself finally for the night on the stone pedestal. It was only half-past six, and as yet not completely dark, but as he had work to do to-morrow he felt that a good night's sleep was the best insurance against fatigue. Despite his boasting about being in perfect condition the climb up the mountain had tired him and he took the precaution to open the little carton of talc and empty it liberally into his socks. From long experience he had learned that a blistered heel could be as dangerous to him as anything could be, and he took the precaution of massaging his feet once he had divested them of the boots which Boris had ordered for him. It was an old walker's trick inherited from the first war, when those unlucky enough to get trench feet were penalized for it.

The bed of soft dark bracken upon which his light sleeping-bag had been unrolled was sweet-smelling and comfortable, though he knew from experience that it must be changed every second day or else it collected fleas—from where he had never managed to discover. He settled himself to doze after having set out his torch and pistol within easy reach of his hand. The massive walls of the cave blotted out all the sounds of the outer world and in the silence he felt his mind slowly clearing as it returned to the incidents of the past few days—so perplexingly rich in the promise of solutions which fate had withheld.

The torturing thought of Vida's death returned once more to worry him; and then—those strange oracular messages which were being passed over the radio every few days to the little groups of *émigré* royalists in Paris and London—what did they mean? He had brought a carbon copy of the messages with him and pondering thus he was tempted to light the single candle in his kit and read them once more before he fell asleep; but he desisted and allowed himself to float downwards along the shallow river of memory to where sleep lay waiting for him like some shadowed pool.

The dial of his watch showed him that it was a quarter to four when next he woke, and he sat up with a start. Some half-irrational prompting seemed to tell him that it was the noise of footsteps which had shaken him into wakefulness. He grabbed his pistol, comforted by the cool feel of the butt, and waited. Nothing. The deep silence filled every corner of the cave, save where a single mosquito droned in the darkness. He was about to lie back again when he heard it—the clumsy scratch of boots on the bank below the cave. It was as if someone had slipped and fallen. He waited now with every muscle tense but nothing further followed so after a pause he slipped on his boots, and taking his torch in his hand went softly to the entrance where he peered through the screen of branches at a fragment of night-sky still full of fading stars.

There was nothing to be seen, and after a further long silence Methuen set aside the branches as quietly as he could and crawled out on to the rock where the great tree cast its black circle of shadow. The hillside was still sleeping innocently under a sky of the palest lavender. He looked anxiously about him but could find nothing which might give him a clue as to the nature of his visitor—if such he was. From somewhere over the hill a cock crowed and its clarion was answered hoarsely from the direction of the monastery. A faint distant rumble proclaimed a train. But all around him the forest scrub and river were utterly silent.

He shivered with a sudden dawn-chill and retraced his steps to the cave where he lit the fire and put some water on to boil, glad of the warmth of the crackling twigs. The noise had probably come from some prowling wolf, he thought, remembering the incident of the night before; nevertheless he must be careful. And his thoughts turned involuntarily to the corpse of the monk lying there by the river behind the next shoulder of hill. It would be unlucky if the old man's murder attracted unwelcome attention to this part of the country and compromised his headquarters. "I suppose to be really sure I should move," said Methuen aloud, yet he knew himself loth to leave so splendid a hideout.

## The Lone Fisherman

He busied himself with setting his temporary home to rights, burying the scraps left over from his meal in the soft earth outside and scouring the utensils he had dirtied the night before. By the time he had done this his water was boiling and he made himself a mug of tea, standing outside to drink it, watching the pale tones of the dawn light creep up from the east. To-day was to be devoted to a patrol of the railway to north and south of the valley, and with this in mind he set off in full fancy dress well before sunrise, crossing the river at the nearest point, and walking swiftly into the forest-clad depression which lay opposite him. He skirted the monastery this time and gazed for a while at the old sawmill by the café where he had once sat and played chess against all comers. It seemed just the same. There was a light burning in one of the windows of the tavern and he could imagine a party of lumbermen downing their plum brandies before setting forth on the day's work.

It took him an hour to reach the point where the main valley intersected that formed by the Studenitsa and here he paused to eat some plums and blackberries which he found in a deserted orchard and to wash his face in a pool. Then he set off in the deep woods which crowned the summit, keeping the valley to his left and pausing from time to time to sweep the river and railway with his glasses. There was no untoward sign of movement save for a couple of lorries full of blue-coated policemen reinforced by a sprinkling of leather-men. They were travelling north at some speed and he judged that they were bound for some collective farm where trouble had broken out, and where they would administer summary socialist justice with their truncheons and handcuffs.

The air on this mountain was light and pure, and though he walked fast he felt full of energy; in fact it was all he could do to keep himself from singing as he walked. He examined the fortress he had seen the day before and calculated that not more than a company of soldiers were based there; the tunnels of the railway, however, which lay some three hundred feet below this eagle's nest, were all heavily guarded and he was careful to use his cover skilfully lest he should be picked up from the opposite canyon by someone using glasses as powerful as his own.

But the farther he walked the more astonishingly peaceful became the landscape. Here and there were men ploughing, and once he saw a caravan of mules setting off down the mountain, but in general there was nothing to indicate the presence of alarms or dangers. Once he ran into an old woman gathering firewood and passed the time of day with her, stopping only to ask her if she had any milk for sale; but her hopeless gesture—raising both hands to the sky—told him more eloquently than words could do how impoverished the peasantry in these parts was. He asked her a few questions which, while they were useful to him, were the kind that any passer-by might ask; and told her that he was walking to Rashka to see his family. "Why don't you walk on the road?" she asked. "It is easier." Methuen gave her a knowing wink and said: "Mother, the road is full of official cars and very dusty."

By midday he had covered several miles without seeing anything to arouse his interest and he lay up for a rest in a patch of maize. He had managed to locate the point where he had jumped out of the car yesterday and also the tree which overhung the road, and out of which he was to toss his report to Porson—unless he chose to wait by the milestone and get a lift back to Belgrade. He calculated that the rendezvous was exactly an hour's walking distance from the cave he had chosen as his hideout.

He set off back to the cave in the late afternoon, but this time he gathered some corn-cobs for his evening meal and almost entirely filled one of his large poacher's pockets with stolen almonds and dwarf-pears. Made bolder by the general peacefulness of the scene he several times left cover to take a promising footpath through those scented fields, and it was while he was crossing a stream by a little wooden footbridge that he came upon a man leading a mule laden with small sacks. Methuen stood aside to let him pass and saluted him gruffly and the man replied in a surly tone. He was a huge ugly brute, dressed in patched and greasy clothes and canvas leggings. A torn straw hat was on his head. Having negotiated the stream he turned to face Methuen and said: "Who are you? You don't belong to us!"

Methuen repeated his story only instead of mentioning Rashka, which lay in the direction from which he had already come, he named another village higher up the mountain. The man's eyes narrowed and he looked furtively about him. "Are you alone?" he said and seemed reassured when Methuen said that he was.

"I have some tobacco for sale," he said in an ingratiating whine.

"Good?"

"The best."

"I have no money."

"What have you?"

"A needle and thread."

The man's eyes widened and a smile came over his face. "A needle!" he repeated and laughed with surprise. "From America," said Methuen sticking to the brief Boris had given him. "I get a parcel every month." The man undid his donkey and from a sack took a great twist—several pounds of contraband tobacco—and pressed it on Methuen saying: "In our whole village there is only one needle, passed from house to house."

This incident seemed to thaw him out and he was disposed to stop and chatter but Methuen was anxious to be on his way. As they parted he called after Methuen: "Be careful up there! There are bad people!" and then he winked and gave a horrid leer. "Is it possible", asked Methuen of himself, "that he takes me for a White Eagle?"

He cut across an orchard and down the slope behind the monastery; altogether he had travelled about seven miles, along the four sides of a square. The body of the old monk still lay under the tree by the river and for a moment Methuen felt a pang of conscience: he should, he supposed, dig a grave for it. But there was no time and no energy over, and a diversion from his central plan might prove fatal. He retired into the cave, where the snake once more sat on duty, and shedding his boots, lit a candle and commenced his brief report for Dombey.

# CHAPTER TEN

## *Footsteps in the Night*

His excursion had given him much more confidence and that evening he permitted himself a rapturous hour of fishing in the dusk before returning to the cave. The trout showed little interest in a Pale Olive Dun but rose nicely to a Winged Standard, though once hooked they showed little disposition to fight so that in half an hour he had caught enough to feed a dinner-party of eight. He tried two of the flies which the Ambassador had tied himself, but without conspicuous success, and he abandoned them regretfully as possibly too highly coloured for their purpose.

The snake too showed the first signs of domestication, for it no longer hissed when he appeared in the cave-mouth, and he was able to walk about with more confidence though he did not dare to shed his boots unless he was actually sitting up beyond its reach on the stone bed he had chosen. His dinner that night was more ambitious, consisting of a grilled trout, two corn-cobs, and some nuts and blackberries: and he ate it beside a roaring fire which lit up the cave with a rosy glare and dispelled the evening damps rising from the river.

It did not take him long to write a brief description of the day's exploration, and to add that he intended to stay on—he did not add for how long. With his report he added a note for transmission to Dombey saying that he was well and that the fishing was excellent. Then, turning aside from these tedious chores, he cleaned his pistol, and after tidying his equipment treated himself to half an hour of *Walden*, revelling in the smooth oracular prose which never wearied him, and which seemed to contain a message which tantalized him without ever satisfying.

"Time is but the stream I go a-fishing in. I drink at it; but while I drink I see the sandy bottom and detect how shallow it is. Its thin current slides away, but eternity remains."

He would have been at a loss to explain why phrases like that haunted him, yet they did, carrying magical undertones which made him repeat them to himself under his breath. And it was particularly when he found himself in a place like this, far from the habitations of men, that he found in this little book a richness and resonance which made him feel at one with the lone American in his log cabin, watching the leaves fall on Walden pond.

He blew out the candle and crawled into his sleeping-bag, repeating another of those oracular phrases like a talisman. "Shams and delusions are esteemed for soundest truths, while reality is fabulous!" Methuen murmured the word "fabulous" twice and wondering what his author could mean slid smoothly into a deep sleep.

Once again he was woken that night by what seemed to him the sound of stealthy footsteps near the cave. The fire had burned down to a bed of soft ash, and his watch marked the hour of three. This time, however, he decided to be more ambitious, and crawling swiftly and smoothly from the cave he slipped down the slope to the water's edge and waited there silently for half a minute before fording the stream and crawling up the hillock opposite. From here he could examine the cave-mouth and the hillside around it with his powerful night-glasses, but the visibility was poor and despite a long watch he could see nothing which might account for the noise. He returned to his bed and spent the rest of the night anxiously dozing and starting up at every sound.

The day dawned cloudy with a touch of damp which heralded a rain-storm, and he occupied himself by examining the country to the north of the cave with the same methodical intentness as he had devoted to the railway the day before. The country hereabouts was knotted up into a chain of rolling hills crested with great forests of beech and here not a living soul met his gaze. The wind rattled and roared on these uplands, filling the melancholy emptiness with the sound of shaken foliage and creaking branches. Once on a neighbouring hillside he saw a line of five men riding on horses with high wooden saddles. They were armed and through his glasses he could distinguish the grey tunics of soldiers and even detect the red star which each bore in his cap. He watched the column move slowly out of sight along the eastern flanks of the mountain opposite. Their movements suggested those of a leisurely patrol which has no determined end in view and Methuen noticed that the leader of the file did not even have his carbine at the ready, but wore it loosely slung over his back. They did not seem to fear an ambush on these empty mountains.

The scenery now became more beautiful than ever, though profoundly lonely, save here and there for a beautiful black squirrel leaping from branch to branch, or a huge brown vulture floating through the azure overhead. The steep slopes over which he now made his way were covered with forest land more varied in its composition. The beech predominated, it is true, but everywhere now his eye picked out oaks and thorns, glaucous ashes, and the bursting fountain-like clumps of birch which grouped themselves along the skyline as if inviting him further into those lawny glades. The dull haze began to lift

under the stimulus of an east wind from the plains as he reached
the highest part of that green plateau and from here he was able
to command an immense view—a stretch of blue contoured
mountains stretching away towards Macedonia with here and
there a silver scribble of river to break up the monotony of the
mass. He studied this landscape carefully and patiently through
his glasses though without uncovering anything more exciting
than a few dust clouds on a strip of road, and a team of mules
skirting the side of what looked like a deserted quarry.

Here he spent some hours resting in the sweet-scented
bracken before turning back to his hideout. It was puzzling
that this plateau should yield no sign of life beyond that single
patrol. He had with him a silk handkerchief printed with a
commando map of the area and he worked out his references
as well as he could, marking the silk lightly with a pencil. He
calculated that in these two days he had explored an area of
roughly five square miles around the cave without finding
anything suspicious. Could it be that all Dombey's reports
were false? Troops of course would move along the valleys
where road communications made for speed; but bandits of
any kind would certainly operate on the hills where the cover
was so good. Why was there no sign of them?

He arrived back at the final spur beyond the monastery by
three and was making his way back to the cave by a series of by
now familiar coverts when it occurred to him to see if the body
of the old monk was still lying where he had left it; he accordingly climbed the next hill from the back, making his way up a
dry river-bed, and appeared in the clump of bushes behind the
tree against which the unfortunate fisherman had been sitting.
His nerves gave a jump of surprise when he saw no sign
of the monk's body under the tree. After carefully looking
about him he rose from cover and raced down the bank to the
river. The body had vanished, and though he searched care-

fully in the grass he could see no trace of footprints. Perhaps the people of the village had come out and fetched the old man in—but if so where were their footprints? He was about to give up his search and return to the river when a speck of black on the water, a hundred yards downstream, caught his eye. He drew in his breath and hastily focused his glasses on the spot. The monk's body lay wedged between two rocks at a shallow place in the river, bobbing and shivering grotesquely in the swift current. Someone had thrown it in—but who?

Methuen arrived back at the cave a troubled man; obviously there was someone moving about in this valley who was more skilful than himself at keeping out of sight; the sense of danger returned, and with it a feeling of hopelessness, for here he was, after all, playing a lone hand in a territory which, while it offered nothing substantial for him to see or do, nevertheless was bristling with hidden dangers. He wondered whether his presence had already been observed by the invisible someone who shared this empty valley with him; perhaps the cave had been compromised? Perhaps. . . . But to-night, at any rate, he must leave the cave and lie up by the roadside in order not to miss the dawn rendezvous with Porson. He busied himself with the second half of his report for Dombey and by the time dusk fell he was ready for the trek back to the road.

He had made out an elaborate shopping list of his wants which included a number of tinned delicacies and even bread, and this he included in his packet, asking that they should be dumped for him the following Wednesday. Then, because he was excited at the prospect of spending the night by the road, and because his restlessness demanded some sort of alleviation, he slipped down to the water and collected his rod, seeing with concern that it showed some signs of rust at the joints. Nevertheless he carried it upstream for fifty yards to where a willow-tree overhung a mossy pool and here he indulged that lithe nervous wrist of his, which could almost make a fly write his initials upon the water.

The evening was cool and the sky had cleared. The fish were indulgent and rose to his hook in an agreeable manner, so that he very soon had half a dozen largish trout beside him on the bank, gasping under his duffle coat. These he packed in moss and leaves, and tied the makeshift parcel with some string he had found in his kit. They would, he calculated, make an annoying present for the Ambassador if only he could get them to Porson safely.

Dusk was settling into evening before he finished packing and hiding his possessions in the cave. He set off across the hill to the Ibar gorge taking a new direction along the wooded crest of the hill above the cave, very much on the alert at this time when visibility was so poor and an ambush so easy to contrive. But his fears appeared to be misplaced for he reached the point where the Studenitsa falls abruptly over the high Ibar gorge without mishap. A half-hour of slipping and sliding down the mossy glades brought him to a point overlooking the road without his having once been obliged to leave cover.

Here he stayed for a while watching the patrols moving along the stone cuttings of the railway track opposite. Above the roar of the river he could hear the noise of voices and here and there a cigarette-point glowed in the gathering darkness. He worked his way along among the saplings and bushes, keeping the road below him until he came to the white milestone. A hundred yards beyond it was the tree into which he must climb beside a gushing spring of mountain water. Here he found a grassy hollow and lay down to doze until dawn.

He must have been more tired than he realized, for he fell asleep, lulled by the delicious cool treble splashing of water on stone, and it was past midnight when he was woken by a swarm of mosquitoes which droned about his ears and seemed able to sting through his shirt. He drew the duffle coat round him and tried to sleep but there was no protection for his neck and ears, and after a little while he gave it up as a bad job. What should he do? He longed to smoke but dared not; and he was alarmed to see how long he had slept. If he once fell asleep he might miss the car altogether. Stretching himself, he decided to climb into the tree now. Why wait? At least in that precarious perch he would be too much on the alert to sleep.

Setting his parcel of fish inside his tunic, and buttoning it over the bulge, he crossed the road and hoisted himself into the tree, climbing along the lower branches until he sat perched over the middle of the road, yet hidden in the dense foliage. Hardly had he done so when he heard the noise of a car and saw the yellow splash of headlights approaching from the south, dipping and vanishing among the curves of the road. "It can't be Porson," he told himself, but nevertheless his pulse quickened with excitement.

# CHAPTER ELEVEN

## *The Rendezvous*

The white diffuse light approached less quickly than he had anticipated, shivering along the dark cliff walls, at times disappearing altogether only to reappear once more round a corner like a glow-worm. He settled himself in the deepest part of the tree's foliage, yet being careful enough to keep an empty space below him into which he could lob his packet should the car turn out to be Porson's. He could hear the engine now more clearly and he decided from the hoarse note of the sound that it was not a touring car but a lorry which was approaching—probably carrying wood northward. As it swept round the last bend, however, it seemed to throw the beams of its headlights almost directly into the tree in which he was perched, silhouetting every leaf in its white incandescence of light, so that Methuen all at once felt completely naked and exposed to view. His eyes, accustomed now to darkness, took a moment or two to get used to the blinding glare; and he kept as still as possible, lest any movement of the foliage should betray him.

But one thing he was profoundly thankful for—his sudden change of position: for the lights penetrated directly into the thicket in which he had been lying before. He would have been forced to beat a retreat into the deeper part of the wood, and

could not have done that without being seen. He was just congratulating himself on his good luck, however, when the lorry
drew to a halt, its headlights still blazing, by the gushing
spring and with a clang the drop-cover at the back opened to
release—not a load of wood alas!—but a company of blue-clad
police which scrambled into the road with weary oaths. For
one second he thought that perhaps he had been spotted and
fumbled for the safety-catch of his revolver, but he was reassured when the men advanced to the spring to drink and
wash themselves; the headlights were switched off, and the
dark was suddenly full of pin-points of red light from cigarettes.

He had caught sight of a small group of leather-men who
were obviously in charge of the party, and who now sauntered
up the road together talking. After a ten-minute halt this small
group returned to the lorry and shouted harsh orders. The
headlights were switched on again and Methuen saw two of
the men in leather coats unrolling a map in the glare. He heard
one say: "We should be in position by dawn to comb this area.
This is where he will be—somewhere within this area," and a
shiver ran down his spine for it seemed to him that they must
be talking about him. "We have time," said one, and at another
order the lorry's lights were again switched off.

The police settled by the side of the road in little groups,
some to lie and doze, and some to talk and argue in low voices.
They were hailed from the rock-cutting over the river, and one
of the leather-men stepped forward to answer the shout.
"Police patrol!" he shouted, and climbing into the lorry,
switched the lights on and off half a dozen times—obviously
a pre-arranged signal.

Methuen was by now acutely anxious, for if Porson should
arrive at this moment it would be quite impossible to communicate with him; moreover, if this patrol should stay here

until daylight he would find himself trapped in the tree for the whole of the next day. His feeling of vulnerability was increased by the fact that he had noticed how heavily armed the police were—with tommy-guns and grenades. It was not much consolation to realize that their presence here in force certainly proved that something was going on in the mountains—the mountains which had seemed to him empty of all life. He wished now that he had not cumbered himself with the heavy parcel of fish and he cursed his own stupidity under his breath.

An hour passed and still the patrol showed no signs of moving; the hands of Methuen's watch pointed to half-past three. The first faint streaks of light had begun to come into the eastern sky. A set of headlights started to blink on the road to the south and he set his teeth—hoping that the next arrival was not Porson. This time, however, it was a lorry full of timber which did not stop.

In the light of its headlamps he caught sight of the small group of leather-coated officers, sitting apart from the main body, discussing something in low tones. Then, as the noise of the lorry boomed into silence along the rock-tunnels he heard to his relief a voice cry: "Attention now! All aboard!" and the night was alive with the noise of boots on stone. The lorry was started up, and after its complement of men had been loaded, someone barked a harsh order. Methuen smiled with relief to hear the whine of the clutch as it engaged, and to see the white blanket of light from the headlights move under him and plunge the tree once more into blessed darkness. The machine lurched raggedly off down the road and he was able to stretch his cramped limbs along the branches.

Silence settled once more over the road and Methuen found himself dying for a drink. He did not dare, however, to climb down from his perch, and lay his face to the icy gushing water of the spring. Its ripple tantalized him, and with an effort he forced himself to ignore his thirst and to concentrate on the gradually lightening landscape before him; the peaks of the mountain gorge were being silhouetted ever more clearly against the lightening sky. It was like watching an etching going through its various states. "Please God," he said under his breath, "tell that young brute Porson not to let it get too light."

The hour selected for the rendezvous was four, and as Methuen watched the hands of his watch creep to quarter past the hour he was once more seized with anxiety lest the contact should not be made. Perhaps Porson had had an accident; the simplest mishap could have delayed him by as much as an hour. Perhaps . . . but his speculations were cut short by the whirr of a car engine coming up fast from the south. In the pale lavender dawn light the headlights looked wan and pale, and he could see the faint plume of dust rising behind them. He gritted his teeth now in an agony of apprehension, preparing himself for disappointment, repeating to himself over and over again: "I bet it isn't Porson. It can't be Porson."

But his heart gave a great leap when he saw a second spurt of dust come round the furthest bend in the gorge, some quarter of a mile behind the first. The seconds ticked away and the headlights played their fantastic game of hide and seek along the dark road. Then, with a roar, the old Mercedes blundered out of the final rock-cutting and advanced towards the spring. The hood was down, and both Porson and Blair were wrapped up against the dawn-chill in weird Balaclava helmets which gave them the appearance of demented airmen trying to get airborne. Porson was grinning elatedly up at the tree, though it was clear that he could not see Methuen among the leaves; Blair looked pale and excited. Methuen conquered a desire to shout aloud to them and as the car slid under him he dropped his parcel with a thud squarely into the back. Dust rose up into the leaves around him. The klaxon hooted twice, and he was just able to see a packet tossed out into the long grass by the white milestone when the second car burst into view. It was crowded with sleepy detectives in trilbies, lying dozing in different attitudes, like a litter of cats, while the radio scratched away with some Hungarian gipsy music relayed from Belgrade.

Methuen lay in the choking dust cloud for a clear minute and a half, listening to the drone of the engines diminishing, and gathering himself together for the next move. He was rather alarmed at the painful cramp which had beset him—for he was a practised *shikari* and had spent many a night perched soundlessly in a *mechaan*, waiting for tiger, without suffering unduly from fatigue. "Must be old age," he said grimly, and looking about him carefully, began to edge his way out of his hiding-place.

Dawn was coming up fast now, and it was with relief that he retrieved the bundle left by the car and took to the deeper woods once more, climbing with steady tireless pace on the moss carpets beside the cataracts and pools of the Studenitsa, refreshed by the spray which blew into his face at every step.

He found a small fern-encircled nook at the top and took a short rest, which gave him an opportunity to examine the contents of the parcel which Porson had dropped him. He saw with delight that some of the items on his own shopping list had already been anticipated. There was a bundle of freshly-baked bread and some olives; two or three tins of meat; and—but this was divination—some soap which he had forgotten to bring with him. There was also a woollen helmet and a further supply of solid fuel. At first there was no sign of a written message but after an anxious hunt he found a thin sheet of paper covered with numerals and recognized with a thrill of pleasure the prearranged code from *Walden*. It would take him a little time to work out, and he addressed himself to the last slope after eating some of the bread and olives from the brown-paper parcel.

All was silent as he crept up the river bank, skilfully fording the stream at the familiar point and sneaking up to the cave-mouth under cover. He had set some twigs over the entrance in a special way so that any chance visitor to the cave must disarrange them, and he saw now with relief that nobody had visited his hideout in his absence. The snake had not appeared as yet, and he lit the fire in the early chill of dawn to make something hot to drink. Then he sat himself down with pencil and notebook and his copy of *Walden* to decipher the message Porson had left him. It took him some time to establish the text clearly, and as it grew under his hand he could not resist an occasional whistle of surprise. There were some new develments of startling interest.

"Spoke to Don in Belgrade by phone-code" it began (Don was Carter) "and have the following for you from the Shop. Submarine has left dockyards and reported in Adriatic. Actress Sophia Maric's suicide announced over radio the morning we left for Skoplje, due to 'overwork'. No news of Vida. Military report sinister activity your area. Three regiments of troops and some police converging on you from Sarajevo, Usizce and Rashka respectively, obviously surrounding mountain-range. Ambassador anxious your return and suggests you hop Wednesday car down to Skoplje rather than wait. Don points out that what up to now has been police activity is becoming military operation including one unit of mortars and six machine-gun sections. Hopes you are not responsible for increased activity. Don cables that no advance made on radio messages except that Professor asks you to bear in mind that in original saga king's birthright was hoard of precious stones."

# The Rendezvous

Precious stones! Machine-guns! Sophia Maric! For a while Methuen's brain was in a whirl. What was to be made of all this reported activity in a landscape which offered not a living soul to the view? The larks were rising from the dewy meadows as he walked outside to think the whole thing over. The landscape slept as if it had been freshly painted by the hand of a master. He yawned as he drank some hot cocoa and read the transcript through slowly. He had still two days before the next rendezvous. How should he spend them? "It is really incredible that I haven't put up anything at all," he told himself despondently. "There must be something to show for all this activity somewhere." But where?

He retired to the cave and slept for a while. At midday, after some food, he set off and walked due west along the range until dusk without result. The quietness of the landscape was no illusion for the wild life of the place told him the same tale. It was completely undisturbed by man. In his despondency he even shot a hare with his pistol, regretting as he did so that he had no receptacle suitable for jugging a creature which has such comparatively large bones. Nevertheless he slung it round his waist in a pocket and carried it home with him to the cave.

That night he slept free from alarms and woke to find that a storm had settled over the valley. The dark sky was suffused with clouds, and lightning played among the pines; the river too had turned white as a scar and was full of drifting logs being whirled down by the current. He spent a joyous hour fishing in the rain before returning soaked to his cave, which was by now as warm and dry as an airing cupboard. Here he disposed his catch, the rosy silvered trout, on moss and counting them decided that he had enough for the day if he was to be penned up by bad weather. "I'm really in danger of overeating," he thought, thinking of the hare which he had hung for the night over his chimney.

# The Rendezvous

The rain slashed and the thunder boomed the whole morning long and he was glad for an excuse to lie up and think of his plans. Despondency gave place now to resignation. After all, he had done his best. If there was nothing to report it was not his fault. He could not be expected to go out of his way to search for trouble. Dombey would have to be content. . . . But, and here he swore under his breath, what were the soldiers doing, converging upon this area from so many directions? Damn it, he could not believe that they were out to hunt for him. How would Dombey ever equate his report with that of the military movements?

He retired to bed early that night and the following morning he set out once more, walking due north; he climbed the high saddle of mountains between this valley and the next, and spent some hours with his glasses combing the fells and downs for signs of movement. In vain. The following day he repeated the same journey only travelling due south this time, vaguely in the direction of Rashka. He encountered a few wood-cutters but nothing else; a gang of platelayers worked in spasmodic fashion on the railway; two fishermen sat immobile on the distant banks of the Ibar. That was all. That was absolutely all.

Wednesday (the day of the rendezvous) dawned bright and clear, and conscience bade him once more repeat the long trudges of the last two days. But he had as yet not decided how to respond to the Ambassador's request. Should he stay or should he return? That was the question. If he were to stay until Saturday he might well take one day off to devote to his passion. "I'll stay," he said after a long interior debate. "Damn it, I must." And once the decision was made his spirits rose again. He wrote a fairly detailed report for Dombey, and then made his way down to the river to find the little screened nook from which he fished in the evenings. As he settled himself he repeated the last words of his report aloud, shaking his head sadly as he did so: "I can guarantee a complete quiet in an area of five miles radius around this point."

It was radiantly sunny and the air was full of summer scents; he leaned easily against a bush, screened from both man and fish, and began to scribble his watery patterns, moving from time to time to explore a new piece of watery territory.

As he worked the polished surface of the river he fell into that pleasant contemplative mood, born of deep thought—but not conscious thought—that anglers and perhaps chess-players also regard as the greatest reward of their efforts. The sun shone brightly in the sky and the woods around were alive with bird-song. In a corner of a pool he discovered once more a special trout that he had sworn to take, and was tempting it to the fly by every means at his command when something caught his glance which made him dive for cover.

He had seen the reflection of someone in the water some ten yards away—moreover the reflection of someone who was holding a tommy-gun to his shoulder in an attitude of alertness. In the same blinding flash of recognition he also recognized that the reflection had been pointing in his direction, though not exactly at him. He pressed himself to the ground, thrusting his precious rod as far into the bushes as he could, and coaxed his pistol out of its sling. His dive for safety had taken him into deep cover and he was confident now that he was out of sight, but so was the unknown. He remembered now noticing that the man wore the grey soldier's tunic and the flat cap with the red star.

All was silent, and after a moment's pause he worked his way quietly back to the shadow outside the cave. The tree was like a great eyebrow in the shadow of which he could squat unobserved and look out upon the bare hillside opposite.

The silence, so ominous now with hidden dangers, possessed him like a drug. He listened to it, gradually sifting it for known sounds like bird-song or the noise of the water: like the ripple of wind-blown foliage and the croak of frogs: sifting it for some other indications, however slight, of trespassers. There had been no mistaking the meaning of that reflection. And he was wondering whether perhaps his cave had been discovered when a burst of rapid fire brought him to his feet.

The foliage danced and shook on the hillside opposite as the spate of bullets struck the branches of an arbutus; and at the same time a figure broke cover and began to run with clumsy zigzag steps across the river bank opposite. "God," said Methuen. The tommy-gunner altered his angle of fire and a jumping rain of bullets cracked the polished surface of the river as they sped after the running man. It was now that Methuen had a dream-like sensation of unreality, for the fugitive was dressed exactly like him in every detail from the moth-eaten fur cap to the heavy peasant boots. It was as if some absurd travesty of himself were being pursued by that hail of bullets over the green sward across the river.

A whistle sounded over the hill. The man in the heavy boots lurched and bounded towards the trees with the bullets kicking up the ground at his heels. "He's done it," said Methuen as he saw him reaching safety; but just as he reached the edge of the wood he staggered and crashed out of sight into a bush. "He's hit." Methuen felt a sense of identification with him. He shrank back into cover as there came the sound of running feet, and a soldier crashed through the undergrowth below the cave, holding his tommy-gun above his head as he plunged into the river in pursuit of the fugitive.

At this moment two more soldiers came over the brow of the hill at the double and they all converged on the spot where the man in the heavy boots had gone to earth. "Only three of them," said Methuen. "Shall I shoot them?" but he restrained so wild an impulse, for the range was by now too great for his weapon. Instead he focused his glasses on the spot and watched in an agony of excitement. The three soldiers were hulking peasant lads and showed little aptitude for tracking their man; nor did they seem to have any officer with them. They walked stolidly through the bushes, making a prodigious noise, and occasionally firing a rapid burst into places which they suspected of harbouring the fugitive.

As they advanced in a ragged line down the hill Methuen started with surprise, for he had seen something else; a head had appeared at the further end of the copse they were beating —the head of the man in the fur hat. He gazed about him quickly, like a snake, and began a slithering sliding movement down and away from that stolid row of grey figures; in a few moments he had put a maize-patch between himself and his pursuers and rose from his hands and knees. But now Methuen could see that he had been wounded for he lurched and staggered, clutching his side, his feet continually giving way under him. He reached the bottom of the dell and started making for the river when his strength gave out and he fell face downward on the grass, breathing in hoarse strangled gasps.

In a flash Methuen was out of cover and down the hill. He crossed the stream and reached the side of the fallen man in a matter of moments. He gripped his shoulder and turned him face upward and saw at once that he had been badly hit; a contorted swollen face stared up at him in fear and anger. "Come," said Methuen, "I'll get you out of this. Can you walk?" But the man was past walking—indeed all but past speaking. His eyes were glazed with pain. He was heavily built but Methuen took him up in a special grip of his own and with a vast expenditure of effort hoisted him slowly across the stream and up the hill. "Hurry!" the man kept whispering. "Hurry!" and indeed Methuen needed no bidding. He was in a sweat of apprehension lest the soldiers return before he reached the cave-mouth.

He achieved the journey safely, however, and carried his burden into the cave where he laid it down on his bracken bed. The man groaned from time to time. He had been shot in the stomach, and Methuen had experience enough to recognize a mortal wound when he saw one. He would not live very long. Nevertheless he busied himself to make him as comfortable as possible and after a swig at his flask the man recovered some colour and was able to speak in a whisper: "Brother," he said, "I was trying to make contact for days, but you did not give the signal. I wanted to be sure it was you." Methuen stared at him and said nothing; but the man went on slowly, talking it seemed, as much to himself as to his rescuer. "I waited for the signal. Now I am dying so I shall tell you the message quickly. Listen." Methuen washed his face in warm water and said soothingly: "I listen. I listen."

"Mules. I got the mules. All of them. They will come over the mountains and must be met at the old border wall on the top of Rtanj. Then you will lead them to Black Peter at the Janko Stone. Tell him to load without delay and start for the coast." His voice tailed away into a mumble and Methuen seized a pencil and jotted down the place-names, excited beyond measure to have discovered something concrete. "No delay," the man repeated. "There must be no delay. The police have smelt a rat. Sixty armed men of the Eagles will join Black Peter at twilight to-morrow and they must march at night without a halt." He groaned again and closed his eyes.

Methuen was wrestling with the momentous meanings which could lie behind this message when he heard voices outside the cave. In a flash he was at the entrance in time to see the three soldiers come over the hill towards him, and ford the river. "He must have gone up here," one was saying in a loud drunken voice. They crashed across the shallows and began to climb the slope towards the cave-mouth. Methuen shrank back, pistol in hand, into the deeper shadow. "Keep silent," he whispered to the wounded man. "They are coming."

They advanced in straggling fashion up the hill, arguing loudly, and came to the knoll below the great tree before one said: "Not up here, surely." The second of the three, whose voice was the loudest, replied: "Looks like a cave up there. I bet you'll find him in there."

It looked like the end of everything; Methuen's only consolation was that he might kill all three without giving them time to "hose down" (in the picturesque army phrase) the cave in which he crouched. He waited grimly, listening to the sound of their heavy boots crunching and slipping outside. Then there was a sigh and a voice said: "It's a cave all right."

It was at this moment that the snake saved the day. It slithered into the sunlit patch at the entrance and took up its usual position, waiting no doubt for lizards to creep out and sun themselves unsuspectingly on the nearby rock-face. Methuen heard it hiss loudly; and the scrabble of boots outside, accompanied by a gasp, told him that the party had recoiled. "Look out!" said a soldier. "The snake."

Another began to laugh. "Well," he said, "he can't be living with a brute like that. Shall I kill it?" There was a long pause during which the snake hissed again. One of the soldiers coughed and said: "There is probably another inside. Don't fire."

They stood irresolutely in a circle, and peeping round the corner Methuen realized that he could drop all three without difficulty. Nevertheless he waited. One took off his cap and scratched his head. Then he said with conviction: "Snakes are unlucky. I'm not going in there. Are you?" The other two laughed harshly and Methuen heard them click on the safety-catches of their weapons. "Nor me," said the one with the loud voice. Then he turned away, adding: "Come on, we'll lose him altogether if we waste time."

In the relief from the tension Methuen heard his own even heart-beats above the noise of their heavy boots retreating. He heaved a sigh and thrust his pistol back into its sling, turning once more to the wounded man. There were one or two vital points to be cleared up. But the man had sunk into a coma from which there was no rousing him and Methuen took the opportunity to write a brief account of this latest incident. "I propose", he added, "to meet the mule-team to-night and lead them up to the so-called Janko Stone—which is a sort of obelisk set up long ago to mark the border between Serbia and Bosnia. It is on the furthest plateau, six thousand-odd feet above sea-level, a barren stretch of mountain which I've studied through glasses but not climbed. I'll try for the Sunday morning rendezvous. By then I should know what it is all about."

His spirits rose now at the prospect of something concrete to do, and he turned his attention to his patient, trying to bandage the gaping stomach-wound, from which a fragment of red intestine was trying to escape, with strips cut from his shirt. He also made a little warm soup and tried to force some between the clenched teeth of the wounded man. In vain. He was tempted to try a surgical repair of the wound with the needle and thread which he had with him and had gone so far as to swab the area of the wound with acriflavin when the man's breathing abruptly changed to a heavy gasping snore punctuated by ghastly hiccoughs. Only his extraordinary physique had kept him alive so long. But now the colour drained from his face and his teeth began to grind as if with cold.

Methuen shook him and tried to rouse him from his coma. It was essential to know not only who he was but also to know the password which would admit him to the headquarters of the White Eagles. But it seemed in vain. Once he opened his eyes and muttered: "Mother . . . It's Marko, Mother," and that provided the only essential clue he was to leave Methuen; for the rest the ghastly breathing continued. "He's dying," said Methuen aloud, and folding those blood-caked hands on the fugitive's chest he repeated aloud the only Serbian prayers he could remember, his voice sounding tremulous and thin in the resonance of the cave. In another quarter of an hour the breathing became feebler and the man died with scarcely a murmur. "So your name is Marko," said Methuen, still tormented by the missing pieces of the jig-saw puzzle. "Marko," he repeated angrily, getting his possessions together, "Marko."

It was by now mid-afternoon and he must hurry if he was not to miss the rendezvous. He hid his possessions as well as he could and set off from the cave at speed, doubling and turning from copse to copse, watching for the soldiers. Mercifully they had disappeared as suddenly as they had first appeared and he reached the gorge without seeing a soul. He raced down the mossy slopes at breakneck speed, and arrived at the road with five minutes to spare. Once more he blessed his luck for there was not a soul about and the rendezvous went off without a hitch. Before the dust of the cars had died away he was already in the ditch gripping the white packet which had been dropped. This time it was in ordinary script and said: "Nothing further to report. Presume you will return so this is unnecessary."

"Presume my foot!" he said in the general direction of the road which Porson had taken. "I'm seeing this thing through." And it was with a savage elation that he climbed out of the gorge towards the sunlight which slanted over the plateau. He had decided not to go back to the cave and risk capture, so he had taken with him everything necessary for the long walk up the central plateau. He rested now for half an hour by his watch, and ate some bread and cold meat from the hare he had cooked. Then, after a long drink, he set off, turning due west away from the cave across the slanting valley, towards the source of the Studenitsa.

He walked now at a slower pace more suited to the journey he had undertaken, and as he walked he once more wrestled in his mind with the various pieces of the jigsaw puzzle, trying to fit them all together into one comprehensible pattern. Certainly the picture had somewhat cleared. It was quite plain that the White Eagles had discovered something of quite exceptional importance in the mountains—treasure of some sort which would enable the Royalists to establish themselves. Therefore they had concentrated as many men as they could around it. It was to be borne westward over the barren karst mountains to the coast where presumably. . . . "Of course," he said aloud, striking his knee with impatience, "the submarine." It was to be got out of the country by submarine. "The King's birthright?" he reflected. "Precious stones? Uranium?" Methuen became increasingly angry with himself for not being able to guess the answer to the riddle. He munched bread as he walked.

Then there was the question of Anson's death; it was fairly clear that Anson was also on the point of solving the mystery when death had caught up with him, though how and in what form it was impossible to say. Certainly the return of the body by the Communist authorities suggested that they were not themselves responsible for it. If Anson had somehow blundered into the headquarters of the White Eagles it was quite possible that they had silenced him without knowing more than that he was a foreign spy.

Yet all the time at the back of his mind there was an irritating feeling that he already knew the nature of the King's treasure, that he had already heard, or read somewhere, something which would give him the answer. What was it? "It's clear, too," he added aloud, "that the leather-men have also discovered something. There is going to be a most almighty battle about it."

He crossed the first shoulder of mountain beyond the monastery and could not help stopping to admire the soft undulating mountain lawn through which his way led by a maze of paths, through fir plantations and groves of mulberry trees. The fresh smell of hay was delicious and in the middle distance he saw the higher slopes dark and feathery with beeches. It was quite hard to imagine that once he crossed the crest he would be far from towns and human habitations. The landscape had the premeditated air of a great formal park and one half-expected to see the gables of some Elizabethan country house peeping through the screen of green foliage at every corner.

The sun was sinking though its warmth still drugged the windless air and on this side of the mountains the flowers and foliage grew more and more luxurious, while the woods were full of tits and wrens and blackbirds. The woods were carpeted with flowers, sweet-smelling salvia, cranesbill, and a variety of ferns. Here and there, too, bright dots of scarlet showed him where wild strawberries grew, and in these verdant woods the pines and beeches increased in size until he calculated that he was walking among glades of trees nearly a hundred feet in height. He could not help contrasting all this peace and beauty with the grim errand upon which he was bent, and which might lead him to sudden death.

He crossed the western slopes of the ridge and began to climb steeply through a pine plantation—pines with long wrinkled arms and shaggy beards of lichen, like patriarchs, awakening in his mind memories of Lapland. Then once again, on the sunny slopes beyond, the pines gave place to beeches— cheerful avenues of sun-dappled arches opening into glades where butterflies fluttered—commas, whites and clouded yellows. He thought of Dombey and smiled grimly. How envious of him Dombey would be if he could see him: Dombey chain-smoking in his gloomy office above the London traffic.

The track he was following now began to ascend rapidly once more and followed a long curve which looked as if it marked the beginning of a water-shed. On the other side stretched the backbone of the mountain-chain, the colour of elephant-skin in the evening light. There was Rtanj, and somewhere in the golden mist beyond it was the Janko Stone. This latter he had heard of on his earlier journey but he had never visited it; indeed only the shepherds with their flocks ever ventured up on to the roof of the mountains, and there were no roads to tempt a traveller.

He rested for a while in the woods, pleased with his progress, for he reckoned to reach the crown of Rtanj well before midnight, which he presumed must be the rendezvous time for the mule-train. At any rate if he were late they must wait for Marko, he told himself; and since Marko was dead. . . . He surveyed the whole range through his glasses but could see nothing of interest. A flock of sheep grazed on the nether slopes of the mountain but he could see no sign of the shepherd, if shepherd they had.

The sun rolled behind a crest and all of a sudden the prospect darkened and flushed red. He set out once more, feeling as if he were the last man on earth, walking in a dream landscape towards a destination he might never reach. Yet he was heartened by his own good spirits and by the fact that as yet he hardly felt tired by the long journey he had made that day. His body was getting into the swing of things, he reflected with relief and pleasure.

Darkness fell as he reached the edge of the great bare upland pasture which marked the beginning of Rtanj, and here he found the whole backbone of the mountain deeply carpeted with a kind of grey-mauve heather of great density. It was as thick as a mattress and though he rejoiced in its beauty he was annoyed to have to slacken his pace, for the going had become much harder. Despite this, however, he calculated that he would reach the crown of the mountain with time to spare.

Once or twice in the eerie half-light he thought he caught sight of figures moving to his left, and he went out of his way to investigate: hoping to meet the mule-team. But each time he was mistaken. A thin slice of new moon came out to keep him company but gave little light. The night was windless though the very lack of wind seemed to create a great rushing vacuum of emptiness up here which teased the ears, making them imagine they could hear the sound of distant voices, or water falling, or the calls of birds which had long since returned to their nests.

From time to time he came upon the great smooth stones, remains of the ancient wall, which had once separated two kingdoms, and touching their smooth surfaces with his hands he could not help thinking that there was something eerie about them. They seemed left over from some forgotten Cyclopean age. He was reminded of Stonehenge. The wall followed the crest up the hills until it reached the final obelisk which had been called the Janko Stone—heaven only knew why. It was a useful marker for him, however, and he was glad to be able to orient himself by these great shattered blocks which loomed up at him through the darkness.

It was well after eleven before he reached the crest of Rtanj and stood looking round him at the dim chain of shadowy mountains around. Ahead, at an even higher elevation, lay the second peak where the Janko Stone stood, and here he descried a fitful beam of light, as from a camp fire. "Well," he said, "the rest is up to the mules." And sitting himself down on a fallen boundary stone he shed his equipment and settled down to a well-earned dinner. He had not realized how ravenous he was, and he made serious inroads upon the small supply of food he had brought with him; worse still, he had made no provision for water, as he had counted on operating in the river country, while this bare upland lacked springs or rivers. He hoped the muleteers, whoever they might be, would be carrying water, and would let him quench his thirst.

Midnight came and went. He stood up on the stone from time to time and raked the darkness with his glasses—which were indeed admirable night-glasses and had been owned by a U-boat captain during the war. But the darkness offered him no clue as to the mule-team. He was worried by the thickness of the grass too: for even a mule-team would be completely muffled by so thick a carpet, and perhaps it might pass him by during the night.

The stone was cold, and the heavy dew penetrated his duffle coat. The hand of his watch pointed to half-past one before he heard—not without incredulity, for it might be a trick of the wind—the creak of girths and the snort of some animal—horse or mule perhaps—in the darkness. He immediately started in the direction of the sound, walking swiftly and bending double so that he would not be seen against the sky.

One hundred yards away from his resting-place there was a deep depression in the ground and here he heard the champing of mules and the low voices of men. He did not quite know in what terms to hail them so he lay on the ground and coughed loudly. At once there was silence, and then after a slight pause a deep voice said: "Ho!" drawing out the sound in a solemn and impressive manner.

"Ho!" replied Methuen, drawing the word out for a full second and letting his voice sink down the register in the same impressive manner. He lay on the ground and waited. Presently a voice quite near him said hoarsely: "Marko? Where are you?" Methuen licked his dry lips and said: "Marko is dead. He sent me to guide the team." There was a sudden click of safety-catches in the darkness followed by silence. Methuen went on: "The soldiers found him near the valley of the Studenitsa river. They shot him."

A second figure must by this time have moved forward towards him in the darkness, for another voice said harshly: "Have you light?"

"Yes."

"Light your own face so that we can see you."

His torch was pretty feeble but it gave light enough; he was still lying down and in the yellowish beam he saw that his interlocutors had been standing up addressing the darkness over his head. Now they knelt and stared long and earnestly at him. "Who are you?" said the deep-voiced one. Methuen rose to his knees and gave his cover-name, adding that he had been sent out by headquarters with a message for Black Peter; on the way he had met Marko by accident, had witnessed his death, and was on the way to deliver both messages to the White Eagles. He himself was a Yugoslav who had emigrated to Paris fifteen years before, he added, and had recently been infiltrated to help with the battle.

The men withdrew and muttered together, while Methuen turned off his torch and waited; he took the extra precaution of moving a dozen paces to his right in the dark. Presently the voices approached again and one said: "Very well. We should get going." Methuen scrambled to his feet and came out to meet the muleteers. He found to his delight that a number had brought water-bottles and other more powerful drinks—plum brandy, the ubiquitous *rakia* of Serbia—and more than one smelt strongly of it. There seemed in all to be about a dozen muleteers and they seemed a fairly well-disciplined lot despite

the smell of *shlivovitz* which clung to some of them, for there
was hardly any talking and chatter among them.

The mules formed up in a long straggling line and the man
who seemed to be in charge of the party came to join Methuen.
He was a bulky-looking Serbian wood-cutter (and Methuen
later was to learn that he was the brother of the dead Marko):
"You must lead now", he said simply, "and become our eyes."

While the daylight held Methuen had taken the precaution
to take a bearing on the Janko Stone with the help of his tiny
oil-compass and Capella which was clear and high in the north-
west. It was to be presumed that the terrain, like that which
they had already traversed, offered no difficulty, being grassy
and soft. Nevertheless it is always nerve-racking to be responsible for the direction of a pack of mules and twelve men, when
you have never traversed the road before: when you are not
certain of the reception you will receive on arrival: moreover
when you have no idea what the password is. . . . So Methuen
rambled on to himself as he climbed into the uncomfortable
wooden saddle of the foremost mule and urged the column
forward with a great show of certainty. Most of the men walked
beside their animals, and after half an hour of torture Methuen
decided that their choice was the right one, and followed suit.

The leader of the party drew up beside him and walked along,
talking amiably in the darkness as they sweated and stumbled
upwards towards the clouds. He lived beyond Rashka on the
mountain range which runs eastwards in the direction of Nish.
"Difficult country to hide in," he said. "We lost many men
to the Communists." (He spat expressively into the darkness
at each mention of the word.) Methuen set himself to draw the
fellow out and was delighted by the ease with which the
peasant, having once given his confidence to him, felt no
further need for reticence.

"Do you think", said Methuen, "the mules will be enough

to transport it?" The peasant shrugged his shoulders and said: "If it is carbon or wood or tea, I can give you an answer. But for gold who can say? Is it big? Is it small? Is it dust?" Methuen stopped in his tracks and gave a snort of sheer surprise which was succeeded by a spasm of furious anger against his own short-sightedness. For he had really known the answer to the problem all the time. Only blind stupidity had kept him so long in the dark. For now, at the mention of the word "gold" he remembered the mysterious disappearance of the gold reserves belonging to the National Bank of Yugoslavia at the outbreak of the war with Germany.

When Hitler's troops poured southward into Serbia some sort of attempt had been made to get the gold reserves away to safety. Those belonging to the largest bank of Yugoslavia, however, had been taken somewhere into south Serbia and—by all accounts—lost. At any rate, during the war both Chetnik and Partisan hunted feverishly for the treasure which both believed to be buried somewhere in the mountains of Serbia. The Germans, and later the Russians, had both shown considerable interest in the matter; but without any result. After the so-called liberation—which turned out to be a worse slavery than ever—the government tried to trace the group which had been put in charge of the bullion when it was taken south in a lorry. But it seemed that they had been murdered by Partisans during the war. Not a soul knew the whereabouts of this large sum of. . . . Methuen whistled to himself. "It *must* be the key to the whole thing," he told himself triumphantly. "At any rate it is the only key which unlocks every door."

Still staggered by his own stupidity he went back over every stage of his inquiry and tested against a single hypothesis: if the White Eagles had located the treasure what would they be likely to do? The answer followed very naturally: try and guard it, try and tell the exiles about it, try and get it out by submarine. . . . The gnomic verses which had been broadcast returned to his mind in the light of this new knowledge and he had no difficulty now in deciphering what the message was which lay behind the words.

But as the corollary of the first question one should ask another; namely, what would the Communists do if they found out about the treasure? The answer was short and ugly: surround the place, wipe out the Royalists, and get it.

"You can see, too," said Methuen to himself sleepily, "that the size of it makes it important. I seem to remember a figure of about fifteen or twenty million being quoted in the newspapers. The Royalists would be rich enough to found their movement on something stronger than faith. One could buy arms and agents. . . ." He understood now the importance that Vida had placed upon the discovery; and understanding that he felt once more how dangerous was his own position, for people with so much to lose would stick at nothing—as witness Vida's own death. Presumably she had been considered a dangerous person, perhaps a traitor. . . .

"I suppose," said Methuen to himself, "I should really go back to Belgrade at once." He turned and watched the dark string of mules on the mountain-side behind him for a moment. "Mission accomplished. Thank you very much." He imitated Dombey's voice congratulating him on having cleared up the mystery and smiled. "A good agent would clear out now," he admitted, "but there is no transport back." He was committed to the adventure.

## CHAPTER TWELVE

## *At the Janko Stone*

They marched onwards until nearly four o'clock, along the back-bone of the range. Then Methuen called a halt for half an hour for he was not only very tired himself by this time: he was also a trifle anxious about the nature of their reception at the Janko Stone. In the darkness, without the right password, they might easily be mistaken for Communist troops and ambushed. He judged it wiser to arrive in the early dawn light when one would be able to see and be seen. Besides, he had no clear idea about the headquarters of the White Eagles; they could not maintain a group on this exposed situation—a plateau open to aerial reconnaissance. There must be somewhere a huge depression in the crown of the highest hill—or perhaps a disused quarry.

The air of dawn was chill, but he slept sweetly enough in his heavy duffle coat, while the mules cropped the grass around his head. Half an hour of sound sleep makes a great difference, and he had trained himself to sleep anywhere, at any time. He woke in time to see the first milky dawn light begin to paint in the furthest range of mountains, and looking back along the way they had come, he felt a mild self-satisfaction at the accuracy of his night navigation. About a mile ahead of them rose the final summit of the range, still wreathed in a thick pinkish mist. They were nearly at their journey's end.

# At the Janko Stone

His long low whistle woke the muleteers, and the straggling line formed once again behind him. They set off at a smart pace now, encouraged no doubt by the thought of a comfortable camp awaiting them with fires and hot food. "You know the password of course," said the old peasant, drawing his mule up alongside Methuen in order to offer him a cut of chewing-tobacco. "That is what is worrying me," said Methuen. "I was given the word 'Wings'; but Marko as he was dying said that they had changed the password again." The man looked at him in consternation. "Aiee!" he said, making a long face. "Will we be shot at?"

"Not if they see the mules."

"The Communists use mules."

"Patience. Let us see."

The ground had levelled off now and become much more broken and boulder-strewn with patches of rough ground breaking through the grass cover, like patches of baldness on a human head. The view from here was indescribably lovely, with mountain-peaks stretching away in all directions, softly coloured by the approaching sunlight and packets of coloured mist. "Soon we will be there," said Methuen, and the cavalcade entered the misty fringe of the crown. From the east, like a premonition, came the drone of aircraft.

Visibility now shrank to a dozen paces, and Methuen stopped every two minutes and gave a long-drawn cry: "Ho!" before moving forward. Apart from this they walked in silence punctuated only by the creaking of girths and wooden saddles.

After a quarter of an hour they heard a sharp whistle repeated three times and from behind a white jutting rock came a hoarse bark of command: "Halt." Methuen halted the cavalcade and walked forward a few paces until the cry repeated and the clicking of safety catches warned him that further enterprise of this kind might prove costly. He accordingly stood still and watched a small band of singularly wild-looking ruffians materialize around him in the mist like spectres. They were all clad in white sheepskin jackets and moth-eaten hats. Some were barefoot. But he could not help noticing that they were heavily armed with efficient and obviously well-maintained tommy-guns.

They said nothing at first but prowled around Methuen and the little knot of muleteers like savage mastiffs, sniffing at them suspiciously. It took them perhaps twenty seconds to finish their examination of the mule-train and then one, wild and bearded, came up and demanded the password. "I don't know," said Methuen, "I come from headquarters and Marko died before he could tell me. Take me to Black Peter, he will understand."

To his surprise this answer seemed to satisfy them for they turned, and with a series of sharp barks and yelps—the noises that shepherds make on the hills to guide their flocks—they led the way through the mist towards the summit. "So far so good," thought Methuen as he surrendered himself to this pack of wild creatures, "at least I shall meet Black Peter."

In a quarter of an hour the mountain levelled off and the mist cleared; and here indeed it was as Methuen had surmised— a large quarry with a network of abandoned workings. Some fifty men were bivouacked in lean-to huts built alongside the steep walls, camouflaged with some skill, and properly drained. The camp was still asleep and their arrival caused a general stirring of pallid faces and beards in these shadowy huts. "The mules," someone said, and the words were repeated in gruff voices all round the camp until they swelled into a roar. "The mules. Thank God we've got the mules."

Their guides had dispersed into the entrance of a tunnel and presently one came running out to Methuen, full of the self-importance that a special mission gives, and to the latter's surprise pointed a cocked pistol at him, urging him fiercely into the tunnel. Methuen made reproachful noises and said: "Brother, what does this mean?" But the only answer he got was a scowl and a wave of the pistol. He put his hands above his head and allowed himself to be marched down the tunnel for some fifty yards. Here he was told to halt, while his guide tapped upon a door set in the wall with his pistol barrel.

"Come in," said an extraordinarily soft and musical voice, and Methuen advanced into a shadowy room—resembling a church—lit by a dozen candles, and with some peeling ikons standing against the further wall. "Black Peter," he said, "I have been sent to you from headquarters."

The young man who stood up behind the table was immensely tall and broad. The steep back to his head, the unswept shock of black hair, and the black beard proclaimed him a Serb. He had cruel dark eyes set very close together and huge hands in which he was trying to crack a walnut. He was dressed in a dirty Russian tunic and trousers tucked into the tops of his dirty boots. He had bad teeth. Beside him, next to a candle which shone rosily on his evil old face, sat an old man in a much-patched uniform. His lean jaws were decorated by a fringe of silver beard, while the head was clumsily shaven in such a way as to leave a long dangling elf-lock at the crown. This Albanian type of hair-style was new to Methuen and he presumed that he must be an Arnaut from the Kosmet.

"You did not have the password?" said the old man in a cracked voice, with an air of insinuation. "Now how could that be?" The young man cracked his nut and began to eat it slowly. As he munched he raised his eyes and let them settle on Methuen's face. It was an ugly moment. Methuen repeated his story; he had been recently infiltrated to help the White Eagles. Headquarters had sent him with a message to Black Peter. *En route* he had met Marko and witnessed his death. The password he had been given was "Wings" but this was apparently old. All this he droned out with as much circumspection as he could, staring down the pistol-barrel of his guard, whose curiosity overcame him so that he stood in front of his charge and stared at him like a yokel.

They looked neither convinced nor unconvinced. The old man stared at his lips all the time he was speaking and at last said: "You are not a Serb." Methuen side-stepped this one fairly easily: "My mother is a Serb, my father a Slovene. I have spent many years abroad." He was obsessed by one fear only: that there might be a radio link between this camp and the town organization which he imagined must be based in a town like Usizce, close to the mountains. So far, however, he could see no trace of such a thing; nor did either of his interrogators make notes. The tall one picked his nails with a knife and said: "Describe how you came." Now Methuen was a thoughtful man and had already bothered his head a good deal in trying to imagine how agents could enter and leave the hill territory. There was only one way that he could imagine and he proceeded to describe it. "I took an ordinary ticket at Usizce for Rashka; I jumped off in one of the tunnels at night, avoided the guard and crossed the Ibar river." Then he held his breath to see whether his guess had proved correct.

The tall young man coughed behind his hand and said in a milder tone. "You see we have to be careful." It was the first time that the temperature had dropped and Methuen took advantage of the fact. "I do not care whether you believe in me," he said earnestly, "but for God's sake believe the news I bring. The Communists are surrounding this chain of hills." He took a step to the table and unrolled a map which had caught his eye. "Here," he said. "Look. There is no time to be lost. You must load the treasure to-night and leave early in the morning."

# At the Janko Stone

This captured their interest and they heard him out in silence. "So," said the old man at last as he followed the rapid tracings of Methuen's finger along the spine of the mountain range. "So they finally guessed what we are doing." The tall young man walked up and down several times with compressed lips; then, in a sudden gust of rage, he stopped and drove the dagger he carried into the table. "It is all their fault," he cried passionately. "I told them not to infiltrate too many men into this area. I told them we would draw attention to ourselves. I told them." The old man clicked his teeth sympathetically and nodded. "Never mind. We will do it yet. Over the mountains and through the *karst* country to the coast."

Methuen asked permission to smoke and lit a cigarette. "I am hungry," he said, "and you don't want my opinion. But I tell you that unless we break through the cordon we will be surrounded and lose the treasure."

Black Peter gave a harsh laugh. "That at least *not*," he said, "for the path runs along the bottomless black lake, and if we can't get it out Tito at least won't get it. That I swear." He made a wide gesture in the air and added: "That at least I swear."

"I'm hungry," repeated Methuen wearily, and with an impatient gesture Black Peter came over to him and said: "I am not convinced of your story as yet." Methuen shrugged his shoulders and replied: "Well, ask headquarters. But if you waste precious time you may find. . . ." His voice tailed away for a new sound had begun to reverberate in the cave—the sound of planes. They were close now and the noise of their engines rippled and boomed among the hills. In the camp outside the tunnel there was a stir. Orders were barked. Feet clattered on the stony corridors. Black Peter opened the door and shouted: "Branko!" A savage-looking one-eyed man shambled into the room touching his forelock and caressing the butt of a revolver which he wore in his belt. "Bring this man some food," said Black Peter. "Quickly."

"I want time," he said, sitting down at the table once more. "I want time to consider." There was a tap at the door and a man in a stained military tunic came in and saluted. "Five planes, sir. They saw nothing."

Black Peter made a gesture of despair. "How could they *help* not seeing," he said. "Go away," he added to the messenger. "Go away"; and in tones of weary resignation he said: "Ignorant peasants, what do they know?"

A table had been cleared in the corner and Methuen was told to sit down and wait for some food, an order which he obeyed with alacrity. The nervous relief at not having committed any major blunders had intensified his hunger and weariness, and placing his folded arms upon the table he leaned his head forward and fell into a sleep which was only broken by the arrival of a bowl of soup swimming with meat and fragments of bread. The drone of voices at the other end of the tunnel had undergone a subtle transformation and now that he was awake once more he realized with a start that Black Peter and the old man were not talking to each other in Serbian any more. They were talking Bulgarian, obviously under the impression that their conversation could not be understood by their guest. Methuen smiled grimly to himself and heard Black Peter say: "No, you always accept things at their face value. Why should headquarters send him separately, since they are sending these men to-night over the mountains? Why could he not have come with them? And the story about Marko's death . . . that's another thing that makes me doubt. . . ." The old man said "Ach!" several times in deprecating tones. "Black Peter sees spies everywhere," he said.

Peter blew a puff of smoke from his nose and said: "And the Englishman?"

"Anyway, he was very obvious."

"Perhaps this one also is an agent."

"Then take no chances. Treat him the same."

The old man raised his right hand and did a graceful little sketch in the air of someone firing a pistol; it was a fluent, graceful little gesture, which Methuen caught out of the corner of his eye as he bent to his soup. He realized with a thrill of horror that they were referring to Anson's death. "At least," said the old man, "Branko will do the job cleanly and efficiently —like the monk." He laughed a small creaky laugh and went to the window—which was blank and did not pierce the rock. In this embrasure, however, an ikon stood and the old man studied it with loving attention while he continued to speak, softly, insinuatingly: "The decision is yours, Black Peter. If you are worried about him let us do away with him. But I think his information is correct. You heard the planes."

Peter sighed and relapsed into Serbian again. "Very well, *barbar*," he said. "But I shall be on my guard," and coming over to the corner of the cave where Methuen still sat eating he clapped him on the shoulder and said: "We accept your story."

"Thank you."

"Thank him," said Black Peter curtly, and leaning forward he rapidly ran his hands over Methuen's coat. With a swift gesture he pulled the pistol from its sling and held it up to examine. Methuen went on with his soup. "It's a new American model," he said. "We have bought some in Paris."

"This is a silencer," said Black Peter.

"Yes."

"I will keep it for myself. You may have mine."

"Very well."

He stood up and faced Black Peter, smiling mildly, but inwardly furious to lose this treasure. "Now," he said, "surely it is time to do some planning for our move to-night."

"You should sleep first."

"Where?"

Black Peter shouted once more for the ruffianly Branko and said: "Take this man and let him sleep until midday. Watch him. Bring him back."

Then he turned aside to his great map-littered table, humming a song.

# CHAPTER THIRTEEN

## Black Peter has Doubts

He slept for a good six-hour spell and the sun was high when he awoke on his bed of straw at the end of a long tunnel. As he sat up and yawned he felt a pair of strong arms gripping his shoulders and in a moment his wrists were tightly tied together behind his back. He turned and stared into the hairy face of Branko his jailor. "What is this?" The old man drew the knots secure and tested them with a grunt before answering with laconic abruptness: "Order."

"But Black Peter said——"

"He has changed his mind. Until we can check on you."

Methuen swore loudly and lay back once more. The old man squatted on his haunches and cut an apple into squares with his knife. He proceeded to eat it noisily. "This will gain you nothing," said Methuen. "Absolutely nothing. Can I talk to Black Peter?" Branko shook his head. "He is busy."

Methuen felt the pangs of a gradually dawning despair; he should, he realized now, never have come up here. He should have been content with the knowledge he had gained. Now all his plans might miscarry unless he could gain the confidence of Black Peter.

He requested and was given a long drink of water; and after some thought he stood up and walked to the mouth of the tunnel. Branko followed his every step. The grassy hollows round the great stone obelisk were alive with men and mules engaged in the various activities of a camp. There must have been a good spring somewhere hereabouts, for a long line of men were watering the animals; others were setting up shelters and lighting fires. Immediately opposite was another hollow tunnel, obviously the entrance to some old abandoned work-ing, and here Methuen saw the flash of yellow light from car-bide lamps. Two sentries stood on guard at the entrance with tommy-guns. Shadows flapped and staggered inside the mouth of the cave and Methuen made out the giant form of Black Peter. "There he is," he said. "I must talk to him." His jailor tried to detain him but he shouldered him aside and walked to the cave-mouth where the sentries barred his way. He called out: "Black Peter! I must talk to you."

The leader of the White Eagles was seated on a wooden chest, deep in conversation with two ruffianly-looking men. "What is it?" he said impatiently, and catching sight of Methuen, "Ah! it is you. Come in." Methuen pressed himself past the cold muzzles of the tommy-guns and walked into the flapping circle of light. "Why am I a prisoner?" he said. "You are not," said Peter gruffly, "but I want to be sure about you. Too much is at stake." He waved his hand vaguely in the direction of the inner tunnel and Methuen saw for the first time the long stacks of wooden crates which he presumed must contain the gold bars. "Is this the treasure?" he said and Black Peter stood up, struggling between his desire for secrecy and an obvious pride. He followed the direction of Methuen's glance and sighed as he said: "Yes."

"Gold bars are heavy," said Methuen.

"I know. But there are other things too. Look here." Black Peter took him gently by the shoulder and piloted him deeper into the cave. It was rather like a wine-cellar. Hanging from a long chain of racks Methuen saw what at first he took to be inner tubes of car-tyres, but which proved on closer inspection to be rubber coin-bandoliers, each designed to carry five hundred gold coins. "I see. Each man will carry something. You can't travel fast, then." A furrow appeared on the forehead of Black Peter. "That is the problem. And look here."

Piled in one corner (as bolts of cloth are piled in the corner of a tailor's shop) he saw what at first he took to be a series of strips of sequin-covered material which glittered like fish scales in the yellow light. "What on earth is it?"

Great blocks of gold coins had been joined together into strips, joined by tiny gold staples. Each piece measured about a square foot and in the centre of each was a hole. "I don't understand," said Methuen and Peter gave a hoarse bark of laughter as he picked up one of these glittering sheets and slipped his head through the hole in the centre. It was like a coat of chain-mail, only made of coins. "Each man will also wear one of these golden shirts; and look, there are others to put over the mules like blankets. Methuen gave a low whistle. "But the weight," he said. "You can't do a good day's march with this." Black Peter looked at him for a moment without speaking. "You will see," he said confidently. "You will see."

There was a ripple of movement outside and the sound of voices. Black Peter cocked his ear and said: "The scouts are coming in. They will confirm your story about the troops. Come."

They left the cave and at once a group of bearded peasants rushed across the grass to Black Peter and began to gabble unintelligibly, waving their arms and flourishing weapons of all kinds. For a moment they were inundated with questions and cries and even Black Peter could understand little of what the men had to say. It was useless calling for silence so with admirable presence of mind he lit a cigarette and sat down on the grass; at once he was encircled by the scouts who squatted round him as if round a camp fire, and fell silent. "Now," said Black Peter, and one felt the authority behind his deep melodious voice, "let us speak in turn so that we see the true picture of events. You, Bozo: what have you to tell?"

One by one he heard them out, puffing reflectively at his cigarette, betraying no concern and no impatience. Then he turned to Methuen, who sat close beside him, still uncomfortably pinioned and said: "You are right. We must move tonight." He dismissed the scouts and sat for a while in deep thought on the grass.

He rose at last and walked to where a shattered fragment of the old wall made an admirable natural dais and climbing on to it, with his back to the cliffside, blew three shrill blasts on a whistle. At once the camp hummed with life, as an ants' nest does if one drops something down it. From all quarters men came running to gather before him, and Black Peter waited for them without any trace of impatience. Methuen could not help admiring his perfect self-possession and calm. When the whole band was assembled silently before him Black Peter stared at them for a full half-minute before beginning to speak. He was obviously a born orator and experienced in his effects.

He began by praising their heroism in facing the dangers of guerilla life in a territory as difficult as Yugoslavia; he reminded them that the journey they were about to undertake would be in many ways the most dangerous and exhausting they might ever make. "The treasure is heavy, we know that. Our march will be slow. And I must warn you that it may be interrupted, for the Communists are approaching this mountain from three sides, hoping to cut us off. One thing we must remember. Usually it is the guerillas who can move fast, and who travel light, while regular troops are encumbered with heavy equipment. But in this case we will be the slow ones, the heavily laden ones. We will be like ants laden with ears of corn too big for them. Therefore we shall need discipline. Therefore we shall need skill in place of speed."

A hoarse murmur greeted him, and he waited for silence before continuing. "Many of you know the route I propose to follow; at the head of each column will be a guide who knows the country well. I think we should avoid the cordon easily if we do not lack courage, and by dawn on Saturday we should reach a mountain path known to nobody which runs above the Black Lake. Then to Durmitor and the *karst.*" Everyone spat with pleasure at this and Black Peter went on in a fusillade of sound. "We shall not lose the King's treasure, that at least is certain. Rather we shall die, rather we shall take it into the Black Lake with us, locked in a death-grip with the enemies who have ruined our country." A hoarse ragged cheer broke out and some of his audience shouted: "Well spoken!" and brandished their weapons.

A grim smile played about Black Peter's mouth for a moment. Then he went on seriously: "One thing makes it difficult for us now—namely aircraft. Some of you saw those planes this morning looking for us. If they should find us they would be able to attack us from the air and who could escape? For this reason I ask you: when the planes come do not all start running about in every direction to hide. Let each man stay absolutely still where he stands. Let him become unmoving as the Janko Stone, for the planes cannot see stillness in men— only movement. This is so important to understand that I have taken an extraordinary measure. Three guards have orders to take up a central position if planes are heard, and to shoot immediately at anyone who is seen moving. Now I don't want anyone to be hurt. But whoever moves endangers the life of each one of us, and he will be shot. Do you agree with me?"

# Black Peter has Doubts

A wild chanting cry went up from the assembled band of ruffians: "Well spoken, Peter!" "Well said, Brother Peterkin!"

He waited once more for silence and then in a crisp and altered tone, added: "That is all I have to say. You have one hour in which to eat and rest, and then we must begin the loading. Each man knows what he must carry and what each mule must carry. To-night we shall be joined at dusk by a party of our own men from the mountains above Sarajevo. We leave at darkness."

"At darkness!" he repeated as he stepped down from the dais and shouldered his way through the press to where Methuen sat on the grass. The ropes had begun to cut into his forearms and he was dying for a smoke. Black Peter stood looking down at him for a moment with a smile. "It is very clumsy," he said at last, "and typical of Branko. Here." He undid the ropes at the back with the aid of his henchman and said: "We'll tie your hands in front. Then at least you can smoke if you wish."

"Am I expected to march like this?" asked Methuen testily.

"Yes."

"I can use a gun far better than most of these ruffians of yours. You may need me."

"If we do we will release you."

Methuen stood up and sighed. Black Peter took his arm and said lightly: "Do not take it too hard. It is a natural precaution. Suppose you were an agent—and I may tell you that we have already had one visitor of the kind. You might escape and take back our position and strength to the Communists in the valley."

"Do they not know it?"

Black Peter started to walk slowly to his own headquarters, taking Methuen familiarly by the arm as he did so and piloting him along. "I don't think they do as yet. But we can't be sure.

## Black Peter has Doubts

We have been out of touch with Usizce for several days—I suppose because of all this increased activity. I think that the Communists suspect something big afoot; but they don't as yet know what. They think we are planning to start a revolution in Serbia. Ach! I'm tired." They had entered the room which served him for a battle headquarters, and he slumped down at the table once more. The old man lay asleep in the corner on a tattered-looking couch. Black Peter uncorked a bottle of plum brandy and placed two small glasses on the table. "Sit," he said, "and drink and let us talk about something else apart from this project of ours. I've been six months up here living like a goat. Pretty tiring I can tell you."

It turned out in conversation that Black Peter was not entirely without culture of a sort. He had been trained as an engineer in both Belgrade and Vienna, and at the outbreak of war with Germany had been in charge of a building project in Bosnia. His wife and child had perished early in the war and he had joined the ill-fated Royalist band of General Mihaelovic which called itself Chetnik, and which had been abandoned to its fate by the Allies. With the disappearance of the Chetnik organization and the murder of its chief by the Communists, Black Peter had gone underground and worked for a spell as a cobbler in Usizce.

Then the *émigrés* in London had started trying to patch together the old Royalist movement from the shreds which remained. Black Peter was called and told of a discovery in south Serbia which set his heart aflame once more. Here was a chance to serve the Royalist cause once more. He spoke with touching simplicity of the dangers undergone and the difficulties surmounted in order to infiltrate a well-armed band into a single mountain area. Many of his comrades had been captured; mistakes had been made. "The gravest mistake has been hurry," he said. "Too many men, too many arms in too short a time. I wanted another six months to do things gradually without awakening suspicion. But they want me to hurry. Always hurry. Now we are in danger, as you know. We may have to fight our way through to the coast."

"That would be impossible," said Methuen. "With the whole army after you?"

"Perhaps. But you do not know the route we are planning to follow. You could not bring an army to bear on us at any place because we travel on the top of the mountains; the only time we come down is to-night, the first valley. The rest of the way you could only bring perhaps two battalions into contact. As far as we are concerned the army can race up and down the roads as much as it wants."

"And at the coast?"

"You are a pessimist," said Black Peter impatiently. "You see all the difficulties; but at the coast, my friend, we have a point of rendezvous so perfect that . . . well, I won't tell you any more. I will only say that there is not a soldier within a dozen miles of our point of embarkation."

All this, which sounded on the face of it utterly fantastic, was in fact plausible—so Methuen at least thought as he saw in his mind's eye the great hairy chain of groined mountains running westward upon the map like a cluster of spiders; the eyries of barren white limestone known as the *karst* which succeeded the heavily wooded and deeply glaciated chain of hills upon which they now were.

"Drink," said Black Peter. "Leave the worries to me." The old man snorted in the corner and muttered something to himself. Methuen smoked on in silence while Black Peter turned his attention to his papers, carefully burning them in a biscuit-box and sifting the ash with a poker before calling for an orderly to take them away. "This pistol of yours is a jewel," he said, taking it up from the table. "I let you keep your glasses as a special favour." Methuen smiled. "Will you tell Branko that?" he said. "Because he has relieved me of them."

Branko was summoned and forced to disgorge his loot, which he did with clumsy reluctance, growling under his breath like a mastiff. Black Peter watched him in silence and then curtly dismissed him. "You see?" he said, turning back to Methuen, "I am a just man, and an honest one."

"And my pistol?" said Methuen.

"That is different. I want it." He gave a harsh laugh and slapped Methuen consolingly on the back. "Never mind. We will see. Who lives longest shall keep it for himself."

It seemed a fair enough solution, though Methuen was already busy with plans for escape. Indeed he was beginning to feel that he had committed a cardinal error in coming to the headquarters of the White Eagles. He should have taken the knowledge gained back to Belgrade with him and not ventured his neck in so risky an exploit. But when he started for the Janko Stone he had not realized that he might find himself a virtual prisoner marching to the coast with a column of armed men, an unwitting target for the attentions of Tito's whole army. His blood curdled when he thought of the Ambassador's face. His only hope was to escape and keep the dawn rendez-vous on Sunday with Porson; yet as things were it was not going to be easy. One false move and the suspicions of his captors would be aroused. That might lead him to share poor Anson's fate. And then, on the other hand, it was absolutely vital that some knowledge of the treasure should reach Dombey and the Foreign Office. All sorts of diplomatic repercussions might be expected if the Royalist movement abroad were suddenly to come into large funds. Policy might have to be altered to meet this new contingency. And if the White Eagles did not get through with their precious freight? If he himself perished with them nobody would be any the wiser. Only sooner or later Mr. Judson's disappearance would have to be accounted for. "O Lord," said Methuen despondently to himself. "I seem to have made an awful mess of things."

They ate their midday meal at a clumsy table in the sunshine outside the cave as Black Peter wanted to keep a wary eye on the loading of his mule-team. They ate slices of fat pork-meat heavily spiced and a good country wine with it. Such conversation as there was was punctuated by interruptions. Orderlies came backwards and forwards with reports sent in by scouts; the guides clustered round for detailed instructions as to the route which they had difficulty in following on the map—being unused to such civilized amenities as maps and compasses. Meanwhile the loading went forward steadily and Methuen could not help but admire the excellent camp discipline which he observed; for method and order this ragged band of guerillas would not have disgraced a regular army unit.

As the light slanted towards afternoon he watched a breathtaking transformation of the men and mules into glittering armoured knights and their caparisoned steeds. The shirts of gold gleamed in the sunlight. The mules at first showed fright as the great blankets of gold coins were thrown over them, but their team-leaders soothed them and gradually accustomed them to the new sensation. Panniers were packed, and the great wooden saddles were heaped with the wooden boxes containing the treasure. Black Peter occupied himself tirelessly with details, walking from group to group, admonishing, cajoling and teasing. It was obvious that the men adored him and would follow him anywhere. He was a marvellous natural soldier, thought Methuen with a touch of envy and admiration. It was amazing to watch the whole band a-glitter in gold coats of mail, leading their glittering animals. Once there was an alarm as the sound of planes was heard; but the sound passed away to the east of the camp without anything being spotted in the sky.

# Black Peter has Doubts

As dusk was falling small knots of armed men began to come into camp from several different quarters of the compass. Each new arrival was signalled by sharp cries and whistles, and some two or three were greeted by Black Peter as old friends.

Methuen had braced himself for the arrival of the escort, for surely among this band was someone capable of detecting the falseness of his cover story; someone from headquarters who would give him away. . . . His anxiety mounted as Black Peter advanced to meet some of these new arrivals, to greet them with affectionate tenderness, kissing their faces and hugging them with bearish enthusiasm.

Methuen walked slowly across the grassy depression and climbed the hillock on the other side from where he could just see the upper part of the Janko Stone. A ring of sentries lay in the grass facing inwards towards the depression in which the camp was situated. Nobody was allowed beyond a certain radius, lest he showed himself in the skyline, and in consequence the whole wild panorama of peaks and mountains was out of sight. Methuen would have liked to climb up as far as the obelisk but he was prevented. Branko walked behind him all the way.

Escape was out of the question. And if he were discovered to be an agent sudden death might follow immediately. Methuen braced himself against an ordeal by interrogation which he felt must soon come. In order to compose his mind he examined an old working in detail, admiring the rich and varied seams of rock which the spades of forgotten men had uncovered; snowy quartz, fragments of rich iron ore glittered over by the scales of mica, pale green serpentine, and dappled jasper. He stopped to pick up a beautiful piece of chalcedony, a network of glittering crystals, which he handed to his jailor, saying: "Look at the riches of this place." Branko grunted doubtfully as he turned the specimen over in his fingers. "And look, there is gold," added Methuen, picking up a piece of fractured iron pyrites with its enticing yellowish gleam. "Gold?" said Branko with interest. "Yes. Here, take it."

These pleasantries were interrupted by a guard who sought them out and said curtly: "Black Peter wants to see you at once in the cave." Methuen drew a deep breath and braced himself. "Now it is coming," he thought as he walked slowly back into the depression which was now swimming with golden warriors and richly caparisoned mules, turned to a dazzle by the last fainting rays of the sunlight.

The cave had been stripped of everything now, and a huge bonfire burned in one corner on which the old man was putting various oddments of equipment and some papers from a wallet. Black Peter sat at the table with a preoccupied air and motioned Methuen to the chair which faced him.

"Well," said Methuen.

"I was hoping some of these people might be able to confirm your story."

"So was I."

"They can't. They've been in touch with headquarters, but not for a day or two; and their field of operations has been around Sarajevo."

"O damn!" said Methuen with a wild joy in his heart which he disguised by holding up his tethered wrists for inspection. "Must I really go about like this? After all the camp is surrounded by sentries. One can't even get up to the Janko Stone to look at the view—much less escape, just supposing I wanted to do so." Black Peter nodded vigorously, and then shook his head once more. "I refuse to take chances," he said with slow obstinate determination.

The room had slowly been filling up with guerillas and it was obvious that he had not more time to spare for Methuen. "Go and get ready," he said. "We march in a little while."

## Black Peter has Doubts

Methuen walked into the starry darkness with a light step. He was overwhelmed with relief. His shaggy janitor now led him to the cave which contained the treasure, and having first untied his hands, slipped a coat of coins over his head. The weight was really staggering—it could hardly have been less than that of a medieval suit of armour. To this was added a double bandolier of coins which rested on his hips. "My God," said Methuen, "one can't carry ammunition as well as this." Branko gave a chuckle. "You won't be expected to use any. As for us we are strong."

"We shall see," said Methuen. The latest arrivals were being loaded with their bandoliers and he noticed that ammunition had been cut to the minimum. It did not argue well for any action they might have to fight on their way to the coast; and food? He had noticed a flock of sheep among the mules and presumed that they would drive a few with them and kill them whenever they camped. "This is going to be some journey," he said soberly and Branko grunted as he replied: "Come along man. Our ancestors did as much and more." Methuen looked suitably shame-faced as he replied: "Yes. It is well said."

Outside the cave in the starlit night the mule-teams had formed up and the camp was bustling with life. Having loaded Methuen up Branko took the opportunity of attaching a long piece of rope to his left arm. This would enable the jailor to walk behind his charge in the night and yet keep a secure hold upon him by means of the rope. They were not going to have him slipping away in the darkness.

Now the melodious voice of Black Peter came at them out of the darkness and a great silence fell. "Men!" said the invisible orator. "Everything is prepared and we are about to set out. I must remind you that none shall speak, and none shall smoke until I tell you. To-night and to-morrow night will be dangerous. Say prayers for your loved ones and for the King in whose name we will perform this exploit or perish."

Branko now led him across the dark grass to join the little group which stood about Black Peter like an unofficial body-guard. "We will march with them in front," he said in a hoarse whisper, and they set their faces to the west, climbing the slopes under the Janko Stone slowly and laboriously, in their coats of mail.

There was a young moon half-hidden by clouds and looking back from the great obelisk Methuen saw the black serpent of the mule-train coiling behind them on that windless mountain. In the darkness around they could see the great clusters of peaks and canyons which surrounded the Janko Stone. The grass was damp from the heavy mountain dew. Black Peter headed the procession with a cluster of armed men round him; then came Methuen and his jailor, closely followed by the leader of the first mule-team.

The path led steadily down towards a watershed and the going was not as even as Methuen had hoped as he stumbled along with Branko tugging at the rope. They walked in complete silence except for an occasional hoarse word of command or a whispered confabulation about their direction among the little party which led the way. For the greater part of the descent they were in the open and it was fortunate that the moon was hidden by clouds, for once or twice they heard the noise of an aircraft overhead—and perhaps the glitter of moonlight on coin might have been visible. Once they had descended into the shadowy watershed visibility became limited and in the inky darkness there were one or two minor accidents—a broken girth, and a man who fell down a steep bank and knocked himself almost insensible with his rifle-butt. But in general their progress was steady and the disciplined behaviour of the men excellent. Methuen kept up as well as he could, glad to be on the move once more, but with his brain swimming with half-formulated plans and hopes which he did not know how to achieve.

They marched through a dark wood and over some rolling dunes of grass reminiscent of the mountain range they had just left. To their left in the darkness they could hear the ripple of water rushing in a stony bed. Once the whole column halted for a while while the scouts went forward to investigate something suspicious. After much whispering they continued bearing sharply to the left and crossing a swift stream at a shallow ford. Methuen was rapidly becoming exhausted both by the weight he carried and by the acute discomfort caused by his pinioned wrists. He repeatedly asked Branko in a whisper if he could talk to Black Peter but each time he was met by a grunt of refusal.

At last, in exasperation, he sat down and refused to walk another step unless he could see the chief. Branko cursed and swore and tugged vigorously at the rope but all to no avail. "Here I stay," said Methuen in a low voice, "until 1 speak to him." The column of mules had halted uncertainly. Branko muttered murderously and drew his pistol which he thrust under Methuen's nose in a threatening manner. But Methuen simply said: "Go on and shoot me, then. I am not moving." While the argument was still going on in hissing whispers Black Peter and his party retraced their steps hastily to see what was the cause of the hold-up. "What is it?" he said angrily.

"He won't move," said Branko.

"Black Peter," said Methuen, "I shall not be able to march with you unless I have my hands free. I am already half-dead. Either you give me a chance to march freely or you can kill me now."

He was in an extremely bad temper by this time, and pouring with sweat. Black Peter paused for a long moment, and then, without a word drew a knife and cut him free. "But be careful," he whispered, and turning to Branko added: "Keep a good hold on the rope."

It was a prodigious relief and Methuen now found that he could keep up with the forward party with comparative ease. They all seemed to be skilled mountaineers, and at almost every stage of the journey they gave proof of their talents, slipping off to left and right of the road on short reconnaisances, using natural cover like born huntsmen. A small group of four scouts had been pushed out about a mile ahead of the party, and each in turn waited to make contact before moving off ahead again; his place was always taken by another. In this way they had an intelligence relay of runners bringing them information about the country they were traversing. These men were the only ones not cumbered with the coin-coats or bandoliers.

It was after midnight when the order came to halt and the party was allowed half an hour of much-needed rest in a shadowy ravine which made an excellent hiding-place. The moon had long since gone, though the sky was soft and lit with bright stars. Black Peter came and sat for a moment by Methuen, wiping his streaming face and asking: "How is it going?" Methuen's good humour had returned with his increased freedom. He had spent his time well, by turning pickpocket and stealing back his compass from Branko. This enabled him to keep an eye on the general direction of the party and he noted with satisfaction that they were walking roughly parallel (though of course at a great distance from) the main road down which Porson must drive on his way from Skoplje to Belgrade.

He still had hopes of being able to escape and reach the road in time for the next rendezvous. But for the moment he was enjoying himself, watching the extraordinary skill with which these mountaineers piloted their mule-team through enemy territory. Once or twice they passed settlements of straw shacks such as shepherds build in the uplands for summer use and at

one of these he noticed a fire burning and the vague outlines
of figures sitting round it. In the clear night air, too, he heard
the monotonous jigging music of stringed instruments. The
column halted in a ravine by a pool and while a scout crept
forward to the settlement the mules were watered and washed
down with as little noise as possible. Presently low voices
sounded in the darkness and they started off once more at the
slow plodding pace of somnambulists.

From here their road began to ascend very steeply and the
going became much more difficult. The soft path turned rudely
to flint under the hooves of their mules and after some time
vanished altogether, leaving them on the wooded side of a
mountain. They toiled their way upward through a jungle of
fern and dwarf-elder, slipping and sliding, and hoisting themselves wherever they could by the help of projecting shrubs.
Progress was slowed up a good deal, and it was with some
relief that they at last reached the beech-glades of the mountain-
top where movement was freer and the surface soft once more.

Through the avenues of great trees they caught an occasional
glimpse of the vistas of mountains which stretched out on
every side of them, but there were no signs of human habitation
anywhere along their path. Dawn was already showing some
signs of breaking behind the backcloth of peaks when they
reached the final peak of the range, and here they were halted in
a fir forest, carpeted with wonderful rich heather already burnt
brown by the summer sun. The order to bivouac was given
and no sooner were the mules safely tethered than each man lay
down and fell asleep in his tracks. Methuen freed himself from
his bandoliers and his coin-coat and followed suit, falling
almost at once into a deep and dreamless sleep.

He woke to find Black Peter shaking him by the shoulder
and saying: "Wake up now. Get under cover." Everyone was
ordered into the shadow of the trees and elaborate precautions

were taken that none of the animals should stray outside the radius of the wood. As the light grew Methuen understood why they were encamped on the crown of a hill which overlooked one of the main roads into Serbia. In this corner of the picture there was also a good deal of activity; frequent cars and lorries rolled along in the dawn light sending up their plumes of dust. They heard, too, a few desultory bangs in the east which might have been the noise of guns, but for the most part the landscape around them seemed as peaceful as a charm.

They lay up here for the whole of that day, eating what food they could lay hands on; those lucky enough to have some bread of their own shared it, and the supply of water was strictly rationed. Black Peter and his little band of sharpshooters lay at the edge of the wood carefully watching the road for signs of military movement. Methuen for his part spent the day dozing. The constant marching and countermarching of the last forty-eight hours was beginning to tell on him, and moreover he had been troubled by a nail projecting from the sole of his left boot. He took ample advantage of the long wait to massage his feet and to get what rest he could. Despite the relative freedom of movement he enjoyed the rope on his arm had begun to annoy him, chiefly because it meant being tethered to Branko and Branko smelt very strongly. He swore that that night he would untie his end of the rope and lash his jailor to some more appropriate bondsman—a mule.

Twice they were visited by aircraft that day, and the second time a reconnaissance plane circled the hill most carefully before flying away to the east. Discipline was perfect and not a soul moved; indeed the cover itself was magnificent and one could lie at ease in the bracken without fear of being detected. Nevertheless these visitations put everyone on the *qui vive*, and Methuen could detect an increase of nervous tension among the men when dusk began to fall. Once more before they set out

162

# Black Peter has Doubts

Black Peter made a short speech reminding them all of the pledge they had taken to win through with the treasure, and Methuen could not help reflecting that this alone betrayed the one weakness of a Balkan soldier—forgetfulness. He must each day be reminded what he is fighting for and exhorted to do his duty.

They set off in the grey dusk and after traversing several shallow ranges all of a sudden reached the foot of a mountain which dominated the whole landscape with its jagged white slopes. The surface had changed again and the noise of the mules' hooves on the loose stones sounded tremendous in the silence. Away to the west they could see a line of bivouac fires —though whether they were troops or shepherds it was impossible to tell. A thin refreshing drizzle fell for an hour and then a wind sprang up and cleared the sky. The young moon looked in on them and they could see the groins and limestone precipices of the mountain they must scale glimmering in the dusky light. They had started on a barren flinty shoulder which climbers would call a glacis; thousands of feet below they could see the tossing woods of Spanish chestnut and wild vine.

At their first resting-point Black Peter came in search of Methuen, full of excitement. "You see now?" he said. "We have not seen a soul, and once we reach the top there is a narrow stone path above the Black Lake which will carry us over to the next mountain. Impossible to ambush us there. It will be like swinging from tree to tree, eh? From mountain-top to mountain-top while the troops walk up and down the valleys." He was tremendously excited. For his own part Methuen did not like it at all; he thought it ominous that so far they had encountered no trace of enemy opposition. But there seemed little point in saying so.

Besides, another and more serious question was beginning to gnaw at him. He must soon make a bid for it if he was to reach the road in time to contact Porson. It was already a long walk as far as he could judge, and a daylight escape would be virtually impossible. He had already experimented with the rope round his arm and found that he could undo it easily enough and tether it to a mule without Branko noticing. But how and when could he slip out of the column and disappear? He would wait, he thought, until dawn when the men were tired.

They trudged on up the mountain for several hours until they reached a large ravine at the top and here, at a bend in the path, an involuntary hoarse cry broke from the throats of the men as they saw the glittering expanse of the Black Lake lying below them. They knew that once they had skirted it the worst part of the journey would be over.

They halted for half an hour and re-formed before entering the gulley which was to lead them by a narrow path along the sides of the lake. The path was of a decent width, allowing two mules to walk abreast for the most part; only in certain spots did it narrow enough to become dangerous. The view from here was indescribably lovely, for they looked down upon the polished surface of the Black Lake from the position of eagles.

Methuen hoped that by dawn they would have finished with this narrow path and emerge into more open country, for his chances of escape were nil under present conditions. Two mules walked ahead of him and two behind, and left no room for someone to squeeze past. The only way out would have been to jump into the Black Lake itself, and that he did not fancy.

Nevertheless he tied Branko to one of the mules without the old man noticing anything and waited for his chance to come. At one of the halts on this rocky staircase Black Peter came back to see if everything was going well. "I am so happy," he said. "I know in my heart that we will get through now. They have missed us."

Who could know the nature of the ambush into which they were walking?

# CHAPTER FOURTEEN

## *The Ambush*

Whenever he thought of the ambush in later years Methuen always recalled the suddenness of it with a shudder. The long march had made them confident of evading capture by the enemy, and their spirits were high as they knew that the path would lead them out on to the crest of a remote mountain-top near Durmitor—far from roads and rivers. Each man felt his spirits rise as he heard his own tramping feet echo against the rocks in a silence punctuated only by the creaking of girths, the occasional snort of a mule, or the faint clink of a weapon touching a coat of coin. Below them slept the lake.

Dawn was already beginning to break, and Methuen was in a fever of impatience to make his bid for freedom. The men marched on in exhausted silence, and as far as he could judge Branko was all but asleep on his feet. At any rate he had not noticed that the rope-end he held was tied to the saddle of a mule.

The path widened now into a rocky defile which gave some space for manœuvre and the press behind grew greater as the leading mule-section halted—perhaps to tighten a loose girth. All at once there came a rapid rattle of sound from over the rocky hillock—like the sound of a stick being dragged across iron railings. That was all. And in the following silence a flock of geese rose off the surface of the lake and circled nervously a thousand feet below. A man coughed loudly, and there came the sound of running feet. Then once more came that ominous rattle, and this time it swelled into a roar, being echoed from three or four different points of the compass. A group of scouts came running, bent double across the rocky corridors and among them Methuen recognized Black Peter waving a tommy-gun. His face was contorted with rage. He shouted a sharp order and the supports surged forward, leaving the mules with only their guards; they clustered round him as he shouted and then loped off to the end of the defile and were lost to sight. Rapid fire now sounded from the entrance and whitish chips of rock began to peel off and fly into the air. It was as if a dozen pneumatic drills had suddenly started up in competition.

Methuen sprang forward and grasped Peter by the arm. "What has happened?" he said and Black Peter suddenly burst into tears of rage as he answered: "They are over the path. We must fight our way out." The rocky cliff prevented any serious estimate of the situation and Methuen shouted: "Come up the cliff and let us see." Black Peter was already giving orders to line up the mules under cover of the cliff. A rush of guerillas swept past them towards the firing-point, shouting hoarsely. "Come," said Methuen in an agony of impatience and seizing Black Peter's arm he pulled him towards the cliff.

Even though the guerilla leader was cumbered by a heavy automatic weapon he climbed like a goat and Methuen had a job to keep up with him. They climbed to the highest spur and cautiously edged themselves between two great rocks from which point they could look down over the crown of the hill. Methuen gave a groan for it was clear that in another five minutes the path would have led them out into the open, on to a wooded promontory. And it was here that he saw, squinting through his glasses, the long ominous grey line of squatting infantry. "Machine-guns," he said gloomily, "and by God!" There was a faint crash and a puff of smoke which sailed languidly into the air while over to the left of their position, on the rocky crown of the next hill, came a jarrying spout of stone and gravel which whizzed about their ears like a choir of gnats. "Mortars!" said Methuen.

"Mortars!" echoed Black Peter. "We must fight our way through. God's death! It's getting light. We must give the word for a general advance."

They rejoined the guerillas on the ledge below. There was considerable confusion of men coming back and others going forward. Several were wounded.

Methuen rushed across the path and into the defile in order to see for himself what things were like at the point of action. As he turned the corner the air swished and whooped about him and he flopped to his stomach and began to crawl. The path debouched on to the crown of a hill and here he saw the scrambling kicking bundle of wounded men and mules. The advance guard were returning the fire of the troops over this barrier but it was quite clear that there was little chance of a break out of the narrow entrance where the noise of the firing was simply deafening. Some of the guerillas had climbed the sides of the gorge to take up firing positions and the noise of their tommy-guns was like the noise of giant woodpeckers at work. Fragments of stone were flying everywhere.

As he lay, pressed against the side of the cliff, he heard the ragged roar of the supports coming up. They surged over him like a wave and burst out of the opening towards the crest where the troops were entrenched. A blinding smoke hung over everything and the noise redoubled in volume. It was impossible to see, but Methuen could imagine the line of charging figures racing down the slope towards the machine-guns, shouting and firing as they ran. "What a party to be caught in," he kept muttering to himself as the seconds ticked away.

A wounded man came crawling back out of the smoke crying something which he could not hear above the roaring of the fusillade. Methuen dragged him to the nearest cover and laid him down beside the path. Then he raced back to the central amphitheatre where the greater part of the mules were. Here confusion reigned. The wounded were lying everywhere groaning and cursing, and the skeleton team of muleteers divided its attention between attempts to quieten the animals and vain attempts to help those who had been hurt. A wave of yellow smoke filled the cave entrance through which occasional figures darted or lurched but it was impossible to know how the battle was going. They were like the comrades of entombed miners waiting at a pit entrance after a heavy fall of rock, thought Methuen grimly; and in the general confusion he shed his bandoliers and coin-coat unnoticed, hoping to retreat down the path and make his way out.

But he had hardly started down the path when a new outbreak of firing from the opposite direction set his pulse racing. Were there troops behind them as well as in front? Once more there came the violent scramble of men running for their lives, and stopping to fire short snarling bursts with their tommyguns before resuming their flight. "We are cut off," said Methuen, and sat down despairingly on a pack-saddle. A panic was about to start when suddenly a majestic figure was seen to materialize from the smoke which blocked the first entrance. A shout went up for it was Black Peter. He walked slowly— with the calculated slowness of a drunkard who knows he is drunk and is elaborately anxious to seem sober. He walked with tremendous circumspection, holding his shoulder with his hand. His face was white and his eyes staring. Methuen jumped forward with a cry of "Black Peter!" but the figure advanced at the same slow speed, giving no sign of having heard.

Black Peter walked towards the group of muleteers like a somnambulist. He drew his whistle from his pocket and slowly put it to his lips to blow a long shrill blast. Once, twice, three times he sounded and a hoarse cry went up for this was the pre-arranged signal which told them that the battle was lost. "Destroy the treasure!" he shouted once, weakly, but his voice was lost in the rattle of firing.

Now Methuen was swept aside by the press of mules which were driven to the edge of the path and pushed screaming into space. This was by no means an easy operation as the poor animals, already half-crazed by the din, were terrified to see the immense drop before them and fought madly to escape, snorting and screaming. Some had to be shot and some clubbed, and Methuen's gorge rose as he saw them plunging into space.

Black Peter had fallen to his knees and Methuen caught hold of the young giant and dragged him away from the mêlée. It was clear that he was dying. His eyes were rapidly glazing and his breath came in harsh gulps. "Black Peter," whispered Methuen as he propped the wounded man's head with a rolled-up coat, "is the action really finished?" But there was not a shadow of response in those dark eyes.

The firing had become thinner and more spasmodic now, though it sounded nearer, and was definitely coming from two opposite quarters. The muleteers were working like fiends, throwing their bandoliers and coats into the Black Lake, and urging the screaming and reluctant animals forward to their deaths with wild yells. But even in the confusion Methuen could not help noticing the methodical way they worked. Each mule was led to the edge; its front legs were worked over the precipice and while one man held it another cut the girth and the ropes binding the treasure with a knife. Then the animal was pushed over, or if it showed reluctance was clubbed.

For his own part Methuen was filled with a sort of blank indecision. What should he do, since the enemy was both before and behind? As always in moments like these when there seemed to be no way out of a dilemma he was careful not to panic, not to start running--but to wait upon events. They alone could show him a way out, if way there was to be. Accordingly he busied himself by making Black Peter as comfortable as he could. He took back his cherished pistol from the leather sling at Peter's hip, and refilled a clip of cartridges. From a discarded parcel of food lying on the path he took a piece of bread and some cheese. Then he started off down the path in the direction from which they had been marching when the attack started. He had gone perhaps twenty yards along the path, picking his way over the bodies of men and mules, discarded ammunition boxes and derelict saddles, when he reached a point where the path made a steep turn and here he could see the tell-tale cloud of smoke which indicated that the rear guard was still putting up a fight. Methuen halted in indecision for it was clear that he would never find a way both through his own men and through the ranks of the Communists.

Then it was that his luck changed abruptly for the better. A dead mule lay wedged between two rocks at the very edge of the precipice with the body of its muleteer lying dead across it. The man had been killed as he was trying to urge the mule over the edge. From the high wooden saddle Methuen saw a long coil of rope which had untied itself and hung dangling over the edge, and all of a sudden an idea occurred to him. Would it be possible to find a way of climbing out of his present predicament by lowering himself down the cliff a good way?

In a second he was lying beside the mule staring down into the gulf, his eyes hunting keenly for some vestiges of a path, or a fault in the rock-face which might give him a foothold. He could not resist a sharp cry of joy, for there, forty feet below, was a narrow path running parallel to the one upon which he now was, a path graven in the side of the cliff face. It is true that it was narrow—a mere shelf of rock above the gulf. But Methuen was by now desperate and prepared to follow his luck wherever it led.

He tested the rope after giving it an extra turn or two round the wooden saddle-frame and then, to make it even more secure, he passed it round a smooth rock projection. It bore him easily: and with a final glance around him he lowered himself gingerly into the gulf with a prayer on his lips, not daring to look down into the depths of the Black Lake below.

In his younger days he had been a rock-climber of promise and this experience stood him in good stead now, for he reached the rocky ledge below in a matter of moments and saw with relief that it did indeed continue along the side of the mountain, though here and there it was blocked by a projecting shrub or a fault. Above him he could still hear the unearthly racket of the battle and from time to time a shower of boulders or a grotesque dummy-like figure of man or mule fell slowly past him and produced a dull thick splash in the lake below. It was strange to see how slowly objects seemed to fall as they reached the level of the ledge upon which he stood, turning over and over and giving the impression of trying to unfold in space as they travelled towards the dark water below. The noise of the firing too, seemed to change into a number of different variations of the same sound; one set of guns sounded like woodpeckers, another crisp as whip-strokes, while from above him where the rear guard was still fighting, the firing sounded like a series of dull cracks and hisses—as of a red-hot poker thrust into water.

He was bathed in sweat and trembling with fatigue in every

limb, yet he set off at a good pace towards the eastern end of the massif. At times he had to travel with his back pressed to the rock, so narrow did the path become; and at others he was forced to climb out of his way in places where the path abruptly ceased. Once he was forced to take the risk of swinging across a gap on a shrub.

In half an hour he had put the sounds of the battle well behind him and the path at last petered out on the side of a hill made of rugged outcrops where climbing was again possible, and he was able to travel upwards towards the mountain-top along a narrow funnel. By the time he reached the top the sun had already risen and the mists were steaming up from the lowland meadows.

He had emerged on the crown of the mountain and could see, with a thrill of relief, that the scene of the ambush lay well to the west of his present position. As he crouched in a rocky hollow and ate some bread and cheese with a ravenous appetite he combed the country with his precious glasses. The battle was still going on among the cliffs of the mountain-top and he could see lines of infantry taking up position among the beech woods which crowned the range beyond.

In the valley below him he saw a long train of mounted troops deploying across the watershed they had crossed the previous day. The whole operation had been a masterpiece of planning and had caught the White Eagles at the most vulnerable point of the whole journey—the last defile which might lead them to Durmitor and safety. There was a small reconnaissance plane in the sky hovering over the scene of the battle. As Methuen watched and considered, his heart came into his mouth for he heard the sound of horses' hoofs from near at hand; up the steep mountain path which had been hidden from him by a fold of rock came a cavalcade of troops in the familiar grey uniforms and forage-caps marked with the red star.

# The Ambush

Methuen flattened himself against the rock and held his breath.

They passed him without seeing him and clattered across the rough paths towards the battle—their weapons at the ready. Methuen drew a breath of relief as he heard their horses' hoofs dying away among the rocky defiles, and he for his part made haste to take the path which would lead him back over the watershed and into the country where—how remote in space and time it seemed—the cave was.

Danger always gave one reserves of unexpected strength he had discovered in the past, and now the narrowness of his escape spurred him on. On the crest of the mountain the cover was not good though the path along which they had so laboriously marched was clearly marked. He forced himself to adopt a regular pace in order not to tire too easily, and every hour he took a three-minute rest during which he checked his course with the compass he had recovered from Branko. A fearful thirst was his only trouble and hereabouts there seemed to be no springs or rivulets; he investigated several ravines which looked as if they might have rivers running in them but without any luck.

Away to the east he could see the great mist-encircled massifs of the range which was crowned by the Janko Stone, and he steered for it, bearing right the whole time so that he could cross the foothills and avoid climbing the central range once more. In this way he hoped to find himself back once more in the valley from which he had started on his journey to contact the mule-teams.

The sun was hot now and he was tempted to shed his heavy coat and hat in order to make his march the lighter, but he thought it wiser to keep these articles for he did not as yet know where he was going to spend the night. At his present pace he calculated that he might reach the cave at dusk—provided he did not meet with any mishap. As far as he could see the countryside was more or less deserted. He caught a glimpse of several roads in the distance and could see the plumes of dust left by wheeled traffic, but it was too far to see clearly.

As far as he could judge the concentrations of troops were in the area he had left behind him, but he took no chances; before crossing each range where the cover was sparse he studied his route carefully. Once he was forced to make a long detour owing to the presence of some sheep and a group of shepherds who sat indolently under a cherry tree, playing on reed pipes—a strangely peaceful and reassuring sound to ears accustomed to the rattle and bark of machine-guns. Methuen listened to them as he crouched under cover in a fir forest and devoured the scanty remains of his bread and cheese.

His detour served a good purpose, too, for it led him to water; he found himself entangled in the debris of a recent forest fire—a steep bank clothed with fern and dwarf elder where the ground was covered with sharp splinters of charred and fractured rock, and where he had to scale high barricades of sooty timber in order to reach a cliff edge from where one could hear the distant ripple of a summer river. He slipped and skidded his way down and was delighted to find a shallow pebbled pool brimming with ice-cold water, and he plunged into it bodily, clothes and all, revelling in the icy sharpness of the water and feeling immediately refreshed.

It was here, while he was drying his clothes, that a large and extremely savage sheep-dog spotted him from the hill-top and rushed down upon him, barking. Methuen scrambled for his pistol and covered the beast with it. He was standing in the middle of the stream on a rock, and he hurled a boulder at the animal as a warning to keep off. But it came on down the bank and showed every intention of attacking him. He shot it with great reluctance, for he knew how valuable dogs must be to the peasantry of this remote countryside. But he could not

# The Ambush

afford to take the chance of being given away; and lest the
dog's owner should be anywhere in the vicinity he gathered
up his possessions and set about climbing the opposite hill in
his squelching and waterlogged boots. It was a full two hours
before his clothes had dried out on his body, and the sun by
this time was baking. Despite his hunger and weariness he was
encouraged to look at the distance he had covered through his
glasses—the long shallow spine of the mountain range which
backed the stony watershed.

Once or twice he saw small isolated patrols of grey infantry
mounted on mules, but they were always a good way off and
he was able to pass them by without being seen. Once or twice,
too, he happened upon a long line of peasant muleteers carrying
wood down to the valleys and was forced to hide in whatever
cover was available. Much of the terrain hereabouts was
planted with firs and beeches, and the dense growth of heather
and fern made hiding easy.

By midday he had reached the second range of mountains
which were crowned by the Janko Stone and he took half an
hour's rest. His feet had begun to hurt intolerably and despite
every precaution he had managed to blister both heels. The
flesh was raw and painful. But now he was on the great shelving
meadow upland with its carpets of thick grass, like coarse
brushed hair, and he started out to walk barefoot, carrying his
boots round his neck, tied with string. This relieved him somewhat and as the going was all downhill he made good time
along the range, his pulse quickening every time he came upon
a familiar landmark pointing the way to the valley of the cave
which he had begun to think of almost as home.

The long fatigue of the journey had begun to make itself
felt and he found himself falling into a pleasant stupefaction as
he walked; it was as if he had detached himself from his body
and allowed it to walk on towards the horizon like an auto-

maton, leaving his mind suspended up here on the windless
pasture land which buzzed with crickets and shone with butterflies. This, he recognized, was the sort of state in which one
became careless and unobservant and he did his best to remain
alert and fully wide awake; but in vain. His mind kept wandering off on a tack of its own.

He thought of the Awkward Shop—the rabbit warren of
corridors in some corner of which Dombey sat, turned green
by his desk-lamp like a mandarin in stage-spotlight, brooding
over his collection of moths; he thought of the companions
who usually accompanied him on missions like the present one
—the Professor with his absent-minded air, and Danny with
his huge hands and yellow hair. And thinking of it all with
nostalgia he cursed himself for a fool to have left it all behind,
to have given way to an impulse. "If I get out of this," he said
aloud, "I'm turning up my cards," and then he laughed aloud,
for he remembered the many occasions when, in the face of
strain and fatigue, he had made himself the same idiotic promise
—a promise which he had never managed to keep.

He had crossed the whole range by now and the sun was
rapidly westering. He had come to familiar country, the soft
shallow hills whose limestone curves foretold the passage of a
dozen mountain rivers towards the Ibar gorge. He was replete
with the excitement of a mission accomplished and the knowledge that he would be in time for the rendezvous at dawn.
The path he followed hugged the banks of a stream rising and
falling along the curvature of the hillside like a swallow and he
walked swiftly and decisively along it, hoping that it would
not be too dark by the time he reached the cave to recover and
reassemble his cherished fishing-rod. The rushing river below
him deadened the sound of his feet on the flinty path. He rested
for a few moments on the bank to drink and bathe his face,
and made a half-hearted attempt to put his boots on, but his

feet were by now too swollen and too painful. It was obvious that he would have to carry on barefoot. He was meditating upon this unlucky chance when a shout from somewhere behind him sent his heart into his mouth. He stood up and turned a dazed face towards the cliff.

A young soldier stood on a spur of rock above him covering him with a carbine. He did not look unduly menacing, and a cigarette hung from the corner of his lip. He waved his hand and shouted: "You there! Come here for questioning." Methuen put his hand to his ear as if he did not hear very well and pointed to the river. "What do you say?" He was thinking rapidly as he moved slowly away from the bank. If there were more troops on the hill behind he was finished. "What cursed luck," he exclaimed involuntarily as he obeyed.

# CHAPTER FIFTEEN

## To Be or Not To Be

The soldier stood nonchalantly with his back to the sun, smoking, in an attitude that suggested lazy indecision. Methuen's eyes took in the grey uniform, the mud-spattered gaiters and ugly boots: the flat cap with its lack-lustre star: and lastly the short repeating carbine of Russian pattern which he held at the hip. "What is it comrade?" he called in a whining tone. The soldier waved the muzzle of his weapon languidly and shouted: "Come here!" in a more imperious tone. His black eyes had a stupid arrogant expression.

It was clear that he was some peasant conscript from a remote country village rejoicing in the possession of a gun. Methuen nodded and said: "I come, comrade, I come," and started to climb the cliff slowly and wearily. His eyes darted hither and thither, attempting to see whether there were other soldiers about; but as far as he could judge this one was quite alone. What should he do? He was almost within pistol-range now. The wisest move would be perhaps to be quite passive and to come in close under the muzzle of the carbine. If he were asked for his identity papers, as he most certainly would be, he could put his hand inside his coat and draw his pistol with one hand while he grabbed the carbine-muzzle with the other. He climbed with an exaggerated slowness up the slope.

# To Be or Not To Be

When he was half-way up he saw an expression of resolute savagery cross the face of the soldier. His mouth depressed itself in a savage grin as, raising the carbine to shoulder-level, he fired at Methuen at almost point-blank range. Even as the latter felt the hot whistle of the bullet pluck the lapel of his coat he leapt sideways and, in less time than it takes to tell, was cowering under the protection of a rock, swearing volubly in a mixture of languages. He was absolutely furious at this dumb treachery.

The earth began to jump and spatter around the rock as the soldier opened up on him, and Methuen with his pistol in hand cowered back against the smooth stone with murder in his heart. He began to feel sorry for the nonchalant young man who was so liberally peppering the landscape with lead. "You wait, you brute," muttered Methuen through clenched teeth, and in his mind's eye he had a sudden picture of Vida.

An interval of silence followed while the soldier smartly changed the clip on his carbine. He was obviously under the impression that his prey was unarmed. In the first gust of firing Methuen had felt a sharp stab of pain in the calf of his left leg and for a moment he had explored this feeling of pain with concern, for he could not afford to be incapacitated at this late stage of the game. Now in the silence he cautiously stretched his leg and was relieved to find that it responded normally enough, though it hurt him considerably.

A second burst of firing followed and Methuen tossed his fur hat down the slope as a distraction before worming himself away to the left to where a clump of bushes afforded excellent cover. Here he drew his breath for a moment before climbing gently up the slope at an angle. The soldier was still staring at the rock behind which Methuen had disappeared, attentively smiling. He had thrown his cigarette away now and had the butt of his carbine pressed to his shoulder.

Methuen took him softly on the sights of his pistol—the ugly backless shaven skull surmounted by the blue cap—and pressed the trigger. There was a loud sniff and the figure lurched out of sight, its disappearance being followed by a ragged bumping and scrambling noise. He had fallen down the cliff and rolled down to the bottom. In the silence that followed the noise of the river welled up once more, and Methuen could hear, above the sound his own laboured breathing, birds singing in the trees across the valley.

He waited for a long moment before he set off running across the now familiar valley towards the cave. The path was sheltered here and he raced along it, pausing from time to time to listen for sounds of pursuit. But the valley had returned to its silent beauty. Once he thought he heard the barking of dogs in the forest, but that was all. His leg was extremely painful now but he did not dare to stop and examine his wound, for he knew from experience that wounds are apt to seem worse than they really are if once one sets eyes on them. That it could not be anything vital he knew for, despite the pain which made him limp grotesquely, the limb could still be used normally enough.

Twilight was already upon him when he struck the main branch of the Studenitsa river and followed its silver windings and meanderings through the mulberry orchards and across the slopes beyond the monastery and sawmill. He was almost blind with exhaustion now and he forded the river with difficulty, staggering as he felt the sucking pull of the water around his ankles. Nevertheless he had enough presence of mind to wait for a full quarter of an hour on the hill opposite the cave, watching the entrance, before he climbed the slope to enter it.

It was extraordinary, the feeling of affection he felt for this fox's burrow which had sheltered him from his enemies; it was almost like arriving home once more after a perilous journey.

Nothing had changed. The snake was not visible, but then it always retired at dusk. The barrier of greenery which he had placed at the mouth was undisturbed. Methuen entered the musty precincts and groped along the stone edges of the sill for the matches which he had placed in a convenient place together with his candle-stump. He lit up and the warm rosy light flickered once more over the veined walls which glimmered like the marbled endpapers of a Victorian ledger.

The dead man still lay on his rude couch of leaves. Methuen hardly gave him a glance as he busied himself in the collection of his possessions. The bed-roll must be sacrificed, but he was not going to lose the other things. He filled his pockets with the most vital of his possessions, and buried the rest in the earth floor. It was too dark and his leg was too painful now to enable him to hunt for his cherished rod. That too would have to be sacrificed, he realized with a pang. He ate a hasty and scrappy meal as he walked up and down. He did not dare to sit down for fear either that he would fall asleep or that his leg would stiffen and prevent him from undertaking the last lap of the journey into the Ibar valley.

Darkness had fallen when he limped out of the cave and with a final glance around him descended the slope to ford the river. He was glad of this, for it increased his chances of escape if he should run into further trouble. By now his route was familiar to him and he had no fear that he would lose his way. His only preoccupation was his wounded leg which had begun to stiffen up in an ugly manner; but he calculated that it was good for an hour's march. A stiff drink had made him feel much better, though he realized that sooner or later the effect of the spirits would induce sleepiness and he was most concerned about this. Suppose he fell asleep and let Porson pass him in the night—at dawn?

It was useless worrying, however, and he plodded on across

the soft meadows with determination. There was a feeble glimmer of light from one room in the monastery and he heard the distant barking of a dog. Beyond the trees by the sawmill he heard the sounds of singing from the little tavern where the peasants were drinking their evening glass of plum brandy. He smiled as he crossed the ridge for the last time and entered the dark avenues of pines to feel the soft ferny floor of the hillside under his bare feet.

He arrived at the road after a journey full of falls and slips, due to his leg, and worked his way along the northern end under cover of the trees. When he reached a point almost opposite the white marker stone where Porson should stop by agreement, he climbed into the ditch and was delighted to find it still dry and full of tall ferns which afforded excellent cover. Here he must lie until the car came for him, and it was characteristic that having won his way so far he should begin to worry about the rendezvous. His sleepy mind began playing tricks with him, telling him that to-day was not Saturday but Friday. He buried his face in the deep grass and, despite himself, fell into a fitful slumber, lulled by the roaring of the water in the valley below him. He had had the presence of mind to slip the leather thong of his pistol round his wrist and to slip the safety catch.

Time passed and the moon rose. He was woken by the whistle of a train which rumbled through the cuttings opposite and disappeared with a succession of shrill grunts and squeaks into the heart of the mountain. It looked more than ever like a toy with its small lighted carriages, and fussing engine. In the silence that followed he could hear the voices of soldiers and platelayers on the railway-line opposite.

His leg had become stiff now, and to ease it he was forced to turn on his back and lie in a more relaxed position. The mosquitoes too were troublesome and Methuen felt the bumps rising on his face and neck from their sharp bites; but he was too far gone with sleep to care, and sinking his head back into the soft bank he fell now into a deep troubled sleep in which the vivid images of the last two days flickered and flashed as if across a cinema screen: Black Peter's glazing eyes, the turning, tossing figures of men in gold coats falling into space, the mule-teams strung out along the mountain like a serpent, the smile on the face of the soldier with the carbine. Then, too, he saw himself picking Branko's pocket, walking along the edge of the cliff, or running bent double among the bracken like a wounded hare. The whole insane jumble of events seemed to have become telescoped in his mind with those other scenes taken from his first days at the cave—the fish rising to his fly, the rain swishing down from the great bare mountains. . . .

It is possible that he would indeed have missed Porson, so deeply did he sleep, had it not been for a lucky chance; for it was already dawn when he was abruptly dragged from his stupor by the rumble of lorries as a convoy burst round the corner and passed the place where he was lying, the yellow headlamps lighting up the cliff-side and the road with their ghastly pale radiance.

He counted seven lorries, and he could dimly see that they were packed with troops and leather-men. They were heading in the southerly direction which must lead them to the nearest road-point from which to climb to the scene of the battle. Methuen breathed a prayer of gratitude as he came full awake, for dawn was fast breaking; and in the choking cloud of dust which followed their passage he rolled once more on to his stomach and settled himself in a position of watchfulness by the road, half-stifled by the dust and petrol fumes.

He had not long to wait. The dust settled slowly and the dawn-light crept along the sides of the hill opposite, scooping great pools of violet shadow in the sides of the mountains. He heard, thin and sweet in the chill morning air, the klaxon of the Mercedes crying down the gorge, and he could not suppress an involuntary cry of joy. "Good old Porson," he said over and over again, every muscle tense with expectation, as he waited for the car to appear around the bend.

A thousand yards away Porson himself was swearing volubly as he drove the old car around the curves of the road. He was in a bemused and shaky condition, having nearly been run down by the convoy of lorries a little further down the valley. In addition to this he had spent time mending a puncture, and had twice been stopped by troops at a road-block, and forced to show his papers. If Methuen was still alive, and if he had managed to reach the point of rendezvous, perhaps he (Porson) was arriving too late? Perhaps there were troops around the white milestone? If so what should he do? His teeth were chattering with cold and excitement as he gradually throttled down the car and slackened speed, while Blair kept a check on their escort through the back. This time they had kept the hood of the car raised and the side-curtains drawn.

They clattered round the last bend and into the cover of the trees when all of a sudden Porson gave a great yelp of surprise for a battered-looking scarecrow with bare feet suddenly plunged into the road by the white milestone, waving its arms. It limped grotesquely and seemed about to collapse under the wheels of the car. "He's done it," said Blair. But for a moment Porson could not believe it was Methuen, so wild and ragged did the figure seem. He pressed the brake and the car slowed down. "Good show!" shouted Methuen in a thin voice and clutching the handle of the door swung himself by a mighty effort into the back of the car, where Blair immediately threw a rug over him.

"My God," said Porson in a shaky voice as he accelerated once more, "Methuen, are you all right?" but Methuen was pressing his cheek to the dusty floor carpet of the car and thinking that he had never felt so glad to hear English voices in all his life. So great was his relief that he was completely bereft of speech. He tried once or twice to say something but only a dull croak came out of his mouth. Perhaps it was sheer fatigue or the dust he had swallowed. But he became conscious now that he was hot, indeed that he had a high temperature.

He heard Porson say: "Just in time", and then he heard the rumble of another convoy of lorries. The two young men were too busy to pay much attention to him for a moment or two. The car was fairly speeding along the road when Porson turned a pale face over his shoulder and said: "Blair, for heaven's sake, see if he is dead?"

Once more Methuen tried to speak but could only utter a dull croak. Blair's white face peered down at him and a hand touched his cheek. "No. He's not dead. He's smiling," said Blair academically, and Porson made an impatient movement. "For goodness' sake, Blair," he said, "get into the back and see if he's wounded."

With an heroic effort, Methuen rolled over on to his back and croaked. "Not dead, Porson, not dead," and Blair, like a man coming out of a trance, suddenly went into action. He gave Methuen a long shaky drink out of a thermos, and climbing over him on to the back seat, examined him roughly for wounds. "I'm all right," said Methuen feebly, glad that he was recovering his voice at last. "My leg is shot up a bit."

Porson let out an explosive breath of relief. "Thank God!" he said, and there were tears in his eyes. "We'd really given you up as lost. The place is swarming with troops and some sort of battle seems to be going on."

Methuen drank once more, deeply, and spilled some water over the crown of his head. It was wonderfully refreshing. "I know," he said, and even *in extremis* he could not prevent a touch of innocent pride creeping into his voice, "I know. It was going on all round me."

Blair's methodical examination had by now reached his injured leg and Methuen began to protest at these amateur ministrations with a vigour which showed that he was far from seriously wounded. "You just leave it alone until we get in," he said. Blair peered at him gravely. "But it's bleeding," he said. "Colonel, it's bleeding. It may need a tourniquet."

He was vainly trying to recall a diagram he had once seen in the *Scouts' First Aid Manual* of how to apply a tourniquet. You took a pencil and a piece of string. . . . He could not remember exactly. Methuen brushed him aside and repeated: "You leave it alone until we get to the Embassy doctor. I've walked a good thirty miles on it and it'll last out awhile."

"But what," said Porson, jumping up and down in the driving-seat in an ecstasy of curiosity, "what has been happening up there in the mountains? Did you find the White Eagles?"

"They found me," said Methuen, "and darned nearly kept me. I've been trotting up the mountains with them, trying to get the Mihaelovic treasure to the coast, believe it or not. But the troops surrounded us."

"Crumbs," said Porson solemnly, "did you really?"

Blair was feeding him slowly and carefully with bread and butter from a paper bag, and after a long gulp of wine Methuen felt sufficiently recovered to prop himself on one elbow. "The puzzle all fitted together very nicely," he said, "once I reached the White Eagles, though they took some finding. They'd unearthed the treasure, you see. We were fools not to think of that."

Porson blew a great blast on his klaxon in order to express his surprise as he said: "Of course. There is a whole file about it which I read a few months ago. What idiots we are. But Methuen, will they get it out?" Methuen smiled sadly—for in his mind's eye he saw once more those toppling kicking figures falling into the gulf of the Black Lake. "Laddie," he said soberly, "there's not a hope in hell. We walked into the neatest ambush you've ever seen. Regular troops. Caught us in a defile."

But it was useless to attempt a connected conversation for he was still far more tired than he himself knew. His voice tailed away into a sleepy mumble. "I'm going to have a nap now," he said, and propping his head on his arm he closed his eyes and felt the great car racing on towards Belgrade. "And I've lost my fishing-rod," he added as an afterthought.

"His fishing-rod," said Blair in accents of pious horror, raising his eyes to the sunny sky.

"His fishing-rod," repeated Porson, wagging his head.

Methuen began to snore.

# CHAPTER SIXTEEN

## *Sorting Things Out*

The staff of the Embassy attended morning prayers in
the gaunt billiard-room and ballroom combined. This
was a custom upon which the Ambassador insisted
under pain of his displeasure. The service was a modest one
and consisted only of a hymn and a short lesson which was
usually read by the Head of Chancery. After this ceremony the
staff trooped upstairs and the servants went about their duties
in the residence.

It was seldom that anything ever happened to disturb the
tranquil monotony of this short service, and on the morning in
question things were going normally enough when the oak
doors at the end parted to reveal the distraught features of the
Sixth Secretary. He seemed full of some important intelligence,
and though the Ambassador frowned savagely at him, he
continued to stand at the door and beckon away sundry members of the staff with a long finger. Sir John was particularly
annoyed by this behaviour as he was reading the lesson himself
this morning, and felt in particularly good voice. The spectacle
of his congregation being lured away one by one was extremely
annoying.

First Duncan the Embassy doctor tiptoed out, and then
Carter. What the deuce did young Porson think he was up to!

With one eye on his text the Ambassador fixed the interrupter with a sombre and disapproving glance which should under normal circumstances have been enough to drive him precipitately out of the room. He was meditating a sharp but kindly reproof to be administered to Porson later in the day when all of a sudden he remembered Methuen. Doubtless all this infuriating interruption concerned Methuen—for was it not? Yes it was! Porson had just returned from. . . .

Sir John beckoned to his Head of Chancery and surrendered the makeshift lectern to him, telling him in a hoarse whisper to continue reading the lesson. Then he too slipped out of the room and turned down the corridor in the direction of the garage. He reached the kitchen entrance in time to see the door into the garage open. Carter and the doctor backed towards him, holding what he took to be Methuen's corpse, while Porson followed, holding its legs. "How is he?" said the Ambassador, fearing for a moment that Methuen had met with the same fate as Anson. He was relieved to hear the corpse groan in realistic fashion as Porson banged his leg on a door.

"Thank goodness!" exclaimed the Ambassador with genuine fervour. And bearing a share of the burden he helped the trio to carry Methuen up a flight of stairs to the neat white infirmary where they laid him on the table and stood back to give the old Scots doctor room. "I'm feeling perfectly well", said Methuen, "except for this leg of mine."

"I'll just get my carving-knife", said Duncan sombrely, "and be right with you."

"My dear chap," said the Ambassador, catching his hand and wringing it. "I can't tell you how glad we are."

"I'm afraid I'm fearfully dirty, sir," said Methuen who had suddenly become extremely conscious of his sweat-stained clothes and his matted hair. He fingered the stubble on his chin apologetically and added: "One gets simply filthy sleeping out."

Duncan was back now with a huge pair of surgical scissors and they carefully peeled his clothes from him while he lay at ease on the white operating table feeling rather pleased with himself. "If I could have half an hour to wash up, sir," he said, "I'd like to report to you, and perhaps Porson would be good enough to draft something for you to see."

"A hot bath with plenty of soap," said Duncan who was examining his leg with an air of disappointment. "You have four wee holes in your legs, Colonel. Some bits of lead in the calf. Some, I think, should be left to lie but there's a wee one here I'll fish out when we've cleaned you up."

They left him now, and while Duncan swabbed his aching leg with alcohol he lay listening with voluptuous pleasure to the noise of the hot bath running next door. He felt his head. "I've got a temperature," he said and Duncan nodded wisely. "Exposure and fatigue. Twenty-four hours in bed. As for your leg . . . I'm going to excavate a wee bit now so hold tight."

Methuen turned over on his stomach and held tight, gripping the edges of the table while the Scotsman probed the wounds, grunting as he did so. This proved to be more painful than anything Methuen had so far undergone and he sank his teeth into the padded pillow in order not to groan.

"There," said Duncan at last, and he heard the tinkle of lead in a basin. "That's two I've fished out. The others can lie awhile. They'll not trouble you. And by the way, Colonel, it's not lead you'll be glad to know, but bits of rock. Were you peppered by a blunderbuss full of odds and ends?" He chuckled comfortably.

"Rock?" said Methuen.

"Aye. Fragments of Bosnia."

He lay in the white bath and soaked himself for nearly an hour while Duncan sat beside him on the bathroom stool,

smoking and asking questions. Methuen felt his tiredness ooz-
ing from his very bones as he lay there. It seemed almost too
good to be true. Then Porson appeared with all the clothing
shed so recently by Mr. Judson and a fat file of telegrams from
Dombey. "Everything has gone wonderfully," he said. "Mr.
Judson has been in bed with 'flu for a day or two, and now he
has sprained his ankle. How soon will he be walking again,
Doc?"

"It's a terrible post this for practice," said Duncan with
genuine disappointment. "He should be up day after to-
morrow. May need crutches for a day or two if the muscles are
seized up. But it's not serious, unfortunately."

"Unfortunately?" said Methuen indignantly.

"Have pity on me," said Duncan. "Apart from an occasional
cough or cold I have nothing to do. I was full of hope when
Porson brought you in. I thought I'd have some real work to
do."

"Selfish fellow," said Porson.

"I'm beginning to feel apologetic," said Methuen.

"Oh, it's not your fault," said Duncan kindly. "You did your
best for us. Lucky you didn't come back on a slab like poor
Anson."

"By the way," said Porson, "you are going to be kept here
to-day. In the state bedroom. The Ambassador's orders. He
wants to have a long talk with you; and you'll presumably want
to do some dictating."

"Yes," said Methuen. "Help me up, will you?"

He was bedded down in some luxury in the bedroom usually
reserved for important visitors after Duncan had given him an
amateurish shave with the Ambassador's own razor. Sir John
himself came flitting in and out every few moments, obviously
most anxious to hear his story and to compose his telegrams to
the Foreign Office. "I don't want to rush you if you feel tired.

Do have a sleep. We can talk this evening. I'll keep a clerk on duty to send anything we need."

"I'd like just half an hour to lie quite quiet and get it all clear in my mind," said Methuen, "and then I can dictate something. Perhaps Porson would take it."

He lay for a while with closed eyes, luxuriating in the feather mattress of the bed, and trying to compose the events of the last few days into a coherent picture; but when Porson tiptoed into the room again he found Mr. Judson sleeping a profound and happy sleep.

They did not disturb him and it was long past teatime when Methuen awoke and rang for the butler. The door opened to admit Sir John himself, wheeling a trolley crammed with tea-things. "Ah!" he said. "So you are awake at last."

"Yes," said Methuen shamefacedly.

Over a cup of tea they talked and Methuen gave a slow and detailed account of his adventure while Porson sat in a corner dotting and dashing into a shorthand notebook. Then he disappeared and left the two men to talk in the twilight. "The drafts will be back soon," said the Ambassador. "And thank goodness we can talk about something apart from shop. Methuen. . . ."

"Yes, sir."

The Ambassador leaned forward, balancing his cup of tea precariously on his knee, and said: "Don't think it frivolous of me, but anything you can tell me about the fishing might come in useful. One day they might relax this ban on travel inside the country and then maybe I should get the chance to try my hand at the . . . what do you call it . . . Studenitsa river."

Methuen smiled and asked for a map and the two of them settled down to one of those delightful and interminable conversations which for anglers is the next best thing to actually fishing a river. Methuen was flattered by the modesty and attention of the great diplomat and, quietly puffing the pipe which he always carried but so seldom smoked, he gave of his best, cross-hatching in the rivers he knew and scribbling a note here and there about more esoteric matters like bait and weather.

Sir John was highly delighted and when Methuen told him ruefully how he had lost his rod his sympathy was so great that he immediately retired to his study and produced his own—a splendid greenheart by McBey—which he forced upon his reluctant guest.

"I really couldn't, sir," he said.

"But you really must. I insist."

"But it's too much," protested Methuen feebly. "I've never owned anything as beautiful and expensive as this. I should be, well, almost shy to fish with it."

"Don't you believe it," said Sir John.

"I don't know what to say."

"Nonsense."

Methuen smiled. "It is by the purest of good fortune that I didn't leave your book of flies behind. I've ticked the two I thought likeliest—though I really didn't have time to experiment in the way I'd have wished——"

But by now Porson was back with the drafts and a note for the Ambassador. Sir John read it and said:

"There's a message just come through on the Agency tapes about that submarine which was supposed to take off the treasure in Dalmatia. Apparently the Italian fleet caught it trespassing in Italian territorial waters, and ordered it into Trieste. It's a poor look-out for the White Eagles."

Methuen sighed. "It was always a tricky and chancy operation. But something tells me they haven't reached the *karst*, let alone the point of rendezvous." Once more in his mind's eye he saw those toppling, turning figures spinning slowly down into the icy fastnesses of the great lake and felt a pang of pain for Black Peter and his band of shaggy ruffians whose devotion to a lost cause had led them to sudden and ignominious death in the fastnesses of Serbia.

While the Ambassador with crisp succinctness dictated his telegrams from the drafts, Methuen ruffled his way through the file of telegrams from Dombey, many of which were already outdated by events.

"What would have happened", he said when the Ambassador had finished, "if we had got through?" and Sir John sighed and shook his head. "It's always difficult to predict but a well-found Royalist movement might have been a serious factor for the present régime."

"But surely that would have been a good thing? These people hate the West."

Sir John took a turn up and down the floor with his hands behind his back. "I'm not sure," he said, "I'm not sure. A number of strange reports have been floating in from various missions about reported disagreements between Tito and Stalin. At times I have been almost led to predict some sort of rupture. Of course I can't go as far as that, but the situation at the moment seems full of unknown factors. We must wait and see. You see, Methuen, at the moment the Russians certainly have influence here but the country is not yet in a Russian stranglehold. It is a willing partner of the USSR, that no one can deny. But if Tito were overturned by any chance the Russians might move troops in."

"But do you think he is detachable?"

"I don't know. I don't know. Not by us perhaps. He is certainly a Communist. But perhaps by factors outside his own control."

"This is very interesting."

"It's all so speculative that I did not think it worth mentioning to you."

## Sorting Things Out

Methuen lay back and puffed smoke up at the painted ceiling of the state bedroom as he considered the bewildering ramifications of conjecture upon which policy must be built. Four months later he was to recall this conversation with a start as the news of the Tito-Stalin split burst upon an astonished world. Now he simply cocked an interested eyebrow in the direction of the Ambassador and waited for him to continue. Sir John rubbed his chin and gazed sombrely at the log fire. "My feeling is that Tito knows he has gone wrong and is far from blind to the injustices of orthodox Communism. He will have to liberalize or lose the support of the people: indeed he has already lost it. He might yet win it back. Who knows?"

"And the Royalists?"

"Another question mark. By the way, there were one or two small points which I wanted to mention. They slipped my mind. This girl Vida."

"Yes?" said Methuen with a sudden fierce constraint.

"She got in touch with Dacic in the town and sent a message through to say that she was still alive and kicking. Apparently the Royalists—the White Eagles—were so alarmed when she asked permission to let you into the secret that they decided to tell you she was dead and, so to speak, slam the door in your face. In the meanwhile there came another interesting development. Her actual employers in the secret police have sent her out to Trieste on a mission of their own. They apparently trust her implicitly, though it's a foregone conclusion that she'll defect once she gets there. I've asked Dombey to make contact through the consular agent there and get her a safe conduct."

Methuen sat open-mouthed during this recital, his heart beating so fast that he felt suffocated.

"Goodness," he said at last, "what a relief."

"I thought you'd be glad."

"Glad?" said Methuen. "More than glad."

# Sorting Things Out

That night he dined at ease and when Duncan came to visit him he was delighted to find that his temperature was back to normal and his leg much less painful. The Scotsman stared gloomily at his patient and said sadly: "You'll be up and about to-morrow. Maybe you won't even need crutches. It's a sad world."

At bedtime there came a congratulatory signal from Dombey, curt and brief as always, followed by orders to return as soon as he felt fit enough. Porson, who had decoded the message, said: "I suppose you'll be burning to get back home. How would you like to go?"

Methuen thought of the long slow train which dragged its way across Serbia and Croatia and said: "I think I'd like to fly, really."

"When?"

"Day after to-morrow."

Porson sighed and closed the file with a snap. "Here endeth the first lesson," he said. "I'll see that they book you a seat on a plane."

Methuen slept soundly that night and woke to a delightful sunny day. Crickets buzzed in the grass on the green lawns of the Embassy. A lawn-mower whirred somewhere out of sight. He found to his delight that his leg, though it was painful, easily bore his weight. Crutches would be unnecessary. He walked up and down his bedroom in order to verify this exciting fact.

# CHAPTER SEVENTEEN

## *Landfall London*

As he stepped from the plane and started to hobble across the tarmac he caught sight of a familiar figure—the outsize figure of Dan Purcell, leaning against the black racing-car which was the pride of his life—and Methuen smiled with pleasure. "Ah!" said the young man. "There you are at last." To an onlooker their handshake might have seemed perfunctory; yet only those who carried out the delicate and dangerous missions of the Awkward Shop knew what one felt on reaching base safely, and Dan's handshake was eloquent. "Danny," said Methuen, "it's good to see you."

"I've brought the car down."

"So I see."

Dan helped him load his luggage into the boot of the Mamba before taking the wheel and letting the black creature prowl into the main road like a panther. "You know," he said, "I was angry that Dombey didn't let us go together. Every time you go off without a bodyguard you get shot up."

"If you'd come," said Methuen drily, "I doubt if we'd either of us have got back. You would have wanted to take on the whole Yugoslav army. My dear chap, Dombey was right. The job was a round one." In the slang of their dangerous trade missions were either described as "round" or "smooth"; the

former stood as a synonym for "difficult", the latter for "easy".
Methuen went on: "It was so darned round it was practically
all circumference. Only a solo could have got away with it.
Just to think of you thumping over the hills, leaving footprints everywhere and blowing your nose in leaves, makes me
shudder. And as for the Prof. . . . he would have caught a chill
at once."

Dan grinned and said nothing. "Anyway," said Methuen,
"when we did discover what it was all about it wasn't all that
important."

"That's what you think. Dombey has been trotting backwards and forwards to the Foreign Office for the last few days
with an air of great self-importance. You had him worried, you
know. He seldom bites his nails and shouts at secretaries."

"He had me worried," said Methuen. "And this time I am
for a long rest; perhaps a permanent rest."

Dan Purcell whistled an air and executed a brisk manœuvre
which carried them over on to the wrong side of the road
round a Green Line bus. The driver expressed his annoyance
with some force and Methuen thought how good it was to hear
once more those Cockney expletives.

"Where is Dombey?" he said. "I'd better report."

"He's waiting for you at your club."

"Well, that is really handsome of him," said Methuen. "He
is so frightfully thoughtful always."

"Yes," said Dan and then laughed wryly. "As a matter of
fact he has got a little job for us. Don't swear so, Methuen."

Methuen swore loud and long. "It's not for a month or so
yet," said Dan soothingly. "Plenty of time to get fit at The
Feathers. The Professor has gone to Finland to lecture on
something, I forget what."

"Well, this time," said Methuen with dogged determination,
"this time I am not going. I've had enough."

"Sure you're not going," said Dan soothingly. "The Professor and I will look after it. I've already told him that. As a matter of fact . . ." he paused for a moment and looked sideways at Methuen, "it's one of the most interesting jobs we've had."

"That," said Methuen, "I've heard before."

"Well, we'll see anyway."

The rest of the journey passed quickly enough. They exchanged the sort of professional talk which to those who knew would have stamped them as members of the most exclusive club in the world. It was mostly about their colleagues of the Awkward Shop. One had gone to China; another had returned from Siam; yet another was finishing a course on explosives which might stand him in good stead in Albania. From all corners of the world the frail network of Dombey's contriving —what he himself had once called "My Giant Cobweb"— shook and vibrated with their messages. In the immense basement room with its shaded lights the duty clerks worked round the clock gathering in their sheaves of telegrams, sorting, typing and clipping. . . .

It was already dark by the time they reached the centre of London and drew up with a masterful swish outside Methuen's club. They left the luggage to the ministrations of the hall porter and Methuen limped inside to collect his mail.

"Wonder if he's here," said Dan as he led the way into the smoking-room. He was.

Dombey sat huddled up in his overcoat at a corner table, staring at a glass of sherry. He looked as he always looked, dilapidated, dishevelled, as if he had had a night out. "There he is," said Methuen.

Dombey stood up to shake hands almost with an air of constraint. "Methuen," he said, "very good show. Hope you are not too badly hurt."

They sat down and Methuen gave them his own account of the mission—somehow more real and actual than those cold bare telegrams which had recorded each stage so objectively. "And the fishing was good—what there was of it," he could not resist adding.

"I told you it would be," said Dombey without turning a hair.

"Moreover," said Methuen, "I made a point of getting away with part of the treasure." In the pockets of his duffle coat he had discovered a couple of gold coins. One of these had already transferred itself to the watch-chain of the Ambassador. The other he now groped for and produced for his chief. "Ah!" said Dombey, "a gold Napoleon. So at least your story was not invented. I sometimes suspect you fellows of making things up as you go along."

"In the past, perhaps," agreed Methuen equably. "But this time: no. And if you want further proof I can produce some authentic rock which lodged itself in my calf. The Professor will bear witness that it is a genuine piece of Serbia."

"Good," said Dombey. "And now I want to take you out to dinner. There is a young woman who is probably waiting at the corner table I've booked, a woman who. . . ."

"Vida!" said Methuen with delight.

"Vida."

"It's a small world."

And now Dombey surprised him by quoting in Serbian, with a fairish accent, the old proverb: "The world is always too small for the large in heart."